ALL
THE WRONG
MOVES

MERLINE LOVELACE

BERKLEY PRIME CRIME, NEW YORK

THE BERKLEY PUBLISHING GROUP
Published by the Penguin Group
Penguin Group (USA) Inc.
375 Hudson Street, New York, New York 10014, USA
Penguin Group (Canada), 90 Eglinton Avenue East, Suite 700, Toronto, Ontario M4P 2Y3, Canada
(a division of Pearson Penguin Canada Inc.)
Penguin Books Ltd., 80 Strand, London WC2R 0RL, England
Penguin Group Ireland, 25 St. Stephen's Green, Dublin 2, Ireland (a division of Penguin Books Ltd.)
Penguin Group (Australia), 250 Camberwell Road, Camberwell, Victoria 3124, Australia
(a division of Pearson Australia Group Pty. Ltd.)
Penguin Books India Pvt. Ltd., 11 Community Centre, Panchsheel Park, New Delhi—110 017, India
Penguin Group (NZ), 67 Apollo Drive, Rosedale, North Shore 0632, New Zealand
(a division of Pearson New Zealand Ltd.)
Penguin Books (South Africa) (Pty.) Ltd., 24 Sturdee Avenue, Rosebank, Johannesburg 2196,
South Africa

Penguin Books Ltd., Registered Offices: 80 Strand, London WC2R 0RL, England

This is a work of fiction. Names, characters, places, and incidents either are the product of the author's imagination or are used fictitiously, and any resemblance to actual persons, living or dead, business establishments, events, or locales is entirely coincidental. The publisher does not have any control over and does not assume any responsibility for author or third-party websites or their content.

ALL THE WRONG MOVES

A Berkley Prime Crime Book / published by arrangement with the author

PRINTING HISTORY
Berkley Prime Crime mass-market edition / November 2009

Copyright © 2009 by Merline Lovelace.
Cover illustration by Michael Gibbs.
Cover design by Rita Frangie.
Interior text design by Kristin del Rosario.

ISBN: 978-0-425-23118-0

BERKLEY® PRIME CRIME
Berkley Prime Crime Books are published by The Berkley Publishing Group,
a division of Penguin Group (USA) Inc.,
375 Hudson Street, New York, New York 10014.
BERKLEY® PRIME CRIME and the PRIME CRIME logo are trademarks of Penguin Group (USA) Inc.

PRINTED IN THE UNITED STATES OF AMERICA

10 9 8 7 6 5 4 3 2 1

*This book is dedicated
to the men and women in uniform
who put their lives
on the line every day . . .
and put their trust in American ingenuity
and technology to keep them safe.*

Acknowledgments

The characters and events in this story are figments of my admittedly overactive imagination but I owe special thanks to several experts who provided real-life details:

To Lieutenant Colonel Jeffrey Sherk, program manager, Tactical Technology Office, Defense Advanced Research Projects Agency, for his advice and counsel. The good stuff is his, the technological goofs all mine.

To Border Patrol agent Martin Hernandez, El Paso Sector, for patiently answering my questions regarding procedures, tactics, weaponry, and what it's *really* like out there on patrol.

And a special thank-you to Dr. Larry Lovelace, my incredibly skilled nephew and ER doc extraordinaire. I can always rely on him to provide gory details when I need them!

CHAPTER ONE

OUR latest test project arrived on-site exactly four days before I got a boot full of decomposing human flesh.

If I'd known that experience lay ahead of me, I would have refused to sign for the piece of equipment delivered that hot August afternoon. I didn't, of course, so I merely stood alongside the collection of eggheads and misfits who comprise my crack test team and gaped at the contraption nestled inside its packing crate.

"Okay, Techno Diva. Enlighten us."

That came from Dennis O'Reilly. Techno Diva is one of the titles he and the rest of the team have bestowed on me, along with Geardo Goddess, Inspector Gadget and several others that don't bear repeating.

"What the heck is it?"

As usual, O'Reilly was the first to speak up. And, as usual, I had no answer.

I'm a program analyst, for God's sake, not an engineer. Between shifts as a cocktail waitress at the Paris Casino in Vegas, I'd earned a BS in management by showing my face occasionally at Party U, aka the University of Nevada, Las Vegas. Okay, I may have shown more than my face. Somehow I managed a passing grade in Risk Management Techniques. No big deal. Who actually manages risk, anyway?

The United States Air Force, I discovered.

Traipsing into that recruiter's office ranks right up near the top of my list of dumb decisions. My only defense is that I was really, really pissed at the time. With good reason, I should add. Two days before, I'd discovered my husband with his jeans around his ankles and his face buried between our neighbor's 38Ds.

True, Charlie and I had pulled into the Tunnel of Love Drive-Through Wedding Chapel on a whim one wild weekend. Also true, it didn't take me long to realize my mistake. I mean, even with bulldogs like Charlie you *do* have to come up for air eventually. But I tend to be a little stubborn. I hung in there for almost six months playing wifey. Obviously I wasn't very good at it.

I dumped Charlie, but I haven't been quite as successful at dumping the United States Air Force. I've tried. Trust me on this. I *have* tried. Don't even get me started on all the things I hate about the military.

Like these ABUs. That's Airman Battle Uniform for those of you who've never had to wear 'em. They're the air force's latest version of haute couture—baggy pants and a loose, boxy shirt in digitized tiger stripes of blues, grays, greens and tans. The fabric incorporates this high-tech near-infrared technology that is supposed to render you immediately invisible. Maybe if the observer is blind or drunk or both.

Then there's the Uniform Code of Military Justice. Did you know dueling is a punishable offense under the UCMJ? Like, who duels these days?

See why I want out?

Sometimes.

The problem is, the air force is an extremely subversive organization. Right from day one, instructors do a number on you in Officer Training School. You're subjected to classes in military history, strategy and tactics. Some left-foot, right-foot on the parade ground. A little this-is-how-we-really-fight-the-war. A few sessions at the firing range. Then they pin two gold bars on you and presto-digito! You're now responsible for the safety and security of the entire free world.

I know it's bull. I also know I'm the last officer you want with a finger on the launch button. Luckily for the safety and security of the free world, I'm a non'er. That's non-sortie producing personnel to you civilian types. Not seriously engaged in combat to those who are.

Yet despite the hassles, despite the ridiculous regulations governing every aspect of my professional life, I can't shake this irritating sense that I—Samantha JoEllen Spade, product of a long line of losers and boozers—am actually part of something important.

God, I hate that feeling!

I hate even more the suspicion that the air force might

be my last chance to change the course of history and make something of myself.

So here I am, a second lieutenant with all of thirteen months' service under my belt, stuck at a test site a few miles outside of Dry Springs, Texas.

Dry Springs is just what its name implies—a collection of crumbling adobe buildings set smack dab in the middle of the desert some eighty miles east of El Paso and the nearest air-conditioned mall. Talk about a crinkly hair on the back end of nowhere! My team and I would pack up and leave in a heartbeat if we could.

What team, you ask? Our official designation is Future Systems Test Cadre-Three. FST-3, for short. I won't tell you my team's interpretation of that acronym. Think odorous bodily functions. Suffice it to say their version will never appear in any official documentation, although you might spot it on some bathroom walls out here in West Texas.

FST-3 is a minute speck in the mysterious bureaucracy known as the Defense Advanced Research Projects Agency, or DARPA. Another acronym. Brace yourself. You'll see more. The military loves to abbreviate and obfuscate.

DARPA is the central research and development organization for the Department of Defense, but don't let the name fool you. DARPA itself does zero research. Instead, it manages selected projects at universities and major research centers. The goal is to aggressively pursue and develop new technologies that might advance military operations.

Now, normally a program manager such as *moi* lolls around in a nice, clean office at DARPA Headquarters in Arlington, VA. I should also point out that most project managers are civilians or senior ranking officers. Due to a slight difference of opinion with my former boss at the Air Force Research Laboratory, however, I was "loaned" to DARPA and put in charge of my little team.

Our mission is to evaluate technologies developed by small businesses or enterprising individuals who don't meet DARPA's threshold for direct oversight. Translation: we play with gizmos and gadgets developed by mom-and-pop businesses or whacko inventors who putter around in their garages at night.

Most of the time FST-3 operates out of a nondescript office at the sprawling army base just outside of El Paso. Once a quarter we go into the field to evaluate items that might, by some wild stretch of the imagination, have potential for military application in rough terrain. Hence our isolated test site near Dry Springs, Texas.

I have to be careful how often and how loudly I complain about being in charge of FST-3, though. FST-1 specializes in cold weather technology and operates out of an igloo in Alaska fifty miles north of the Arctic Circle. FST-2 battles alligators for space on a hump of sawgrass somewhere in the south Florida Everglades.

Back to my little team. In recent months we've evaluated inventions that ranged from the improbable to the downright ridiculous. But this one . . .

"What is it?" O'Reilly threw at me again.

I shot him an evil look and consulted the paperwork

handed to me by the crew who'd unloaded the crate. "This is the project Harrison Robotics wants us to evaluate."

Our usual methodology is to review submissions and choose items to test well before we go into the field. This was a last minute addition pressed on us by a friend of a friend of an uncle of DARPA's chief scientist. Or was it the uncle of a friend of a friend? Whatever. The weird-looking result was staring us in the face.

"They call it an Ergonomic Exoskeletal Extension," I read. "EEE for short."

Exoskeletons aren't new. Even I know Berkeley University first developed a lower body exoskeleton they called BLEEX way back in '04. But this guy . . .

My gaze swung back to the contraption nested in foam inside the packing crate. Metal braces formed its legs. Additional braces comprised a set of arms. These extremities were connected to a computerized spine. At the top of the spine was a circular headpiece bristling with wires, probes and a face-shielding visor.

"Geez," I muttered. "Damned thing looks like an Erector set having a bad hair day."

The female standing next to O'Reilly let out the snorting neigh I now know is her brand of laughter. Took me a while to figure that out.

"We should call it EEEK." She whinnied. "Not EEE."

EEEK, which rhymes with geek, which is the most generous term one can apply to Dr. Penelope England. Unlike me, Pen aced every one of the classes leading to her two PhDs. Very much like me, she doesn't deal well with persons in authority. Her problem is that she's smarter than ordinary mortals by a factor of, oh, a thousand or so. Mine is that I have a slight tendency to mouth off.

"What are we supposed to do with it?"

O'Reilly again. He also has a mouth on him. Five-two, with orange hair and glasses encased in nerdo black frames. He swiped at the perspiration dripping from his pudgy chin.

I wasn't in much better shape. I, too, am cursed with red hair. Mine is several shades darker than O'Reilly's bright pomegranate, thank God. My late, unlamented ex used to call it dirt red. I prefer cinnabar. And my eyes are a deep, melting chocolate, *not* muddy brown.

Luckily, I don't have your typical redhead's complexion. After I burn and peel a few dozen times, I acquire a semblance of a tan. Only on the patches of skin revealed by my ABUs, of course. Out of uniform, I look like a scalded raccoon.

In it, I'm usually swimming in sweat. Like now. Doing my best to ignore the torrent coursing down between my breasts, I consulted the project sheet again.

"Apparently," I announced after perusing several convoluted paragraphs, "one of us is supposed to strap him- or herself into the exoskeleton and go for a twenty-mile run. In full combat gear. Carrying a sixty-pound pack."

With perfect syncopation, the other four members of FST-3 took a step back. Their feet thumped the dry earth, and their interest in EEEK evaporated as quickly as the scant quarter inch of precipitation that had fallen on Dry Springs so far this year.

"Full combat gear," O'Reilly echoed, his carroty brows soaring above his glasses. "Sixty-pound pack. Sounds like a job for an active duty military type."

My glance zinged to the only other military member of my team. *His* zinged to the purple smudge of mountains in the distance.

We played the waiting game. Ten seconds. Twenty.

"Well, Sergeant Cassidy?"

All right. So I caved. I usually do in face-offs with Staff Sergeant Noel Cassidy. A Special Ops noncom with two tours in Iraq under his belt, he was assigned to FST-3 after beating a charge of lewd and lascivious acts with an underage female.

(There's that Uniform Code of Military Justice again. I'm telling you, it's a piece of work!)

Cassidy's attorney got him off by proving that the underage female he solicited—Cassidy, not the attorney—was actually a he-male well past the age of consent. Sergeant Cassidy would have much preferred a jail sentence. His steroid-and-muscle-bound masculinity has yet to recover from the shock of messing around with a drag queen. As he reminded me when he finally met my determined stare.

"You know my shrink hasn't cleared me for return to full duty."

"She would, if you'd haul yourself up to Fort Bliss."

Fort Bliss is our home station. Three-point-four zillion acres of desert straddling the Texas/New Mexico border. Host to the army's armor and air defense artillery training centers. And FST-3. The main post itself isn't bad, but there's nothing blissful about *this* remote corner of the post unless you're a Gila monster or diamond-back.

"You've missed the last two appointments," I reminded the sergeant.

"I'll schedule another for next week."

"You'd better make this one."

"Yes, ma'am."

I scowled but couldn't bring myself to come down too hard on the guy. After all, the sight of Charlie boinking our neighbor messed *me* up enough to land me in uniform.

"All right." I signed the acceptance sheet and gave it back to the driver. "Let's haul this contraption inside. If and when we figure out how to work the thing, I'll climb aboard and take it for a spin."

FST-3 includes two PhDs, a software genius in the person of O'Reilly, and Sergeant Cassidy, who's racked up more than twelve years of service. Throw in my admittedly mediocre academic credentials and relatively few months in uniform, and you'd think we would have sufficient collective smarts to decipher EEEK.

You'd think wrong.

It took several days, a slew of emails, countless phone calls and the belated arrival from Phoenix of a rep from Harrison Robotics before we could make sense of the schematics. All the while the weird-looking piece of equipment stood in a corner of the CHU that served as our test facility.

Excuse me. That's C-H-U, pronounced choo. It's short

for Containerized Housing Unit. Our site has five of 'em. Two are linked together to form our test and administrative center. One serves as a combination rec room, dining facility and workout area. The latter is used exclusively by Sergeant Cassidy, by the way. The rest of us wouldn't be caught dead on a Universal Gym.

The remaining two CHUs constitute our sleeping quarters while forward deployed, e.g., stuck out here in Dry Springs. The three guys occupy one. I share the other with Pen. Unfortunately, she snorts and whinnies while asleep as well as when she's awake.

I think I mentioned that we're pretty much at the bottom of the DARPA food chain. The thing is, even DARPA's rejects are state-of-the-art. That's where the "advanced" in Defense Advanced Research Projects Agency comes in, you see. As a result, our test lab is crammed with enough computers and high-tech instrumentation to re-orbit the International Space Station.

Our test engineer is a skinny, nervous twitch by the name of Dr. Brian Balboa. Naturally, we immediately anointed him "Rocky" but I challenge you to find anyone less Sylvester Stallone-ish. Rocky isn't as out-there brilliant as Pen, but he's darn good at making all those black boxes of instrumentation sing. Remind me to tell you sometime why he's no longer assigned to DARPA Headquarters.

Even Rocky had trouble with EEEK's computerized components, however. And the more frustrated my team became, the more the contrivance smirked at us. I kid you not. With its head full of wires, crossed arms and casually bent knees, all it needed to complete an air of sardonic amusement was a cigarette dangling from its lips.

"Look."

As agitated as the rest of us, the Harrison Robotics rep stabbed a finger at a monitor. He was bald as Britney Spears during her weird phase and at least two hundred fifty pounds heavier. His name was Benson, Al Benson. My team had instantly dubbed him All Bent.

"You folks have to stop thinking of these as machine parts and . . ."

"They *are* machine parts."

That came from O'Reilly. Naturally.

All Bent scowled and directed his comments to me. "We designed the exoskeleton as a natural extension of the human body."

"Just out of curiosity," I asked, "how many human bodies has it extended so far?"

"Several."

He didn't quite meet my eyes. Not a good sign.

"Including yours?" I wanted to know.

"Well . . . No."

"Why didn't Harrison Robotics send us someone with hands-on experience?"

All Bent squirmed and provided a reluctant answer. "One of our engineers broke a leg when a brace failed. Another slammed into a concrete wall at full speed. He's still on medical leave. But we've worked out the bugs in the power unit," he rushed to assure me. "You'll be in complete control at all times."

I may not be the sharpest pencil in the box, but I'm no dummy. I know how many billions DARPA pours into the civilian sector to develop new technologies. Harrison Robotics was a small firm. Until now, the company had specialized in computerized artificial limbs. EEEK would take them into the much broader—and far more profitable—arena of direct combat support. Naturally they'd brush aside little things like broken legs and head-on collisions with concrete walls in pursuit of Big Bucks.

On the other hand, if their device lived up to its hype, maybe it *would* increase the capability of our war fighters. The robotic legs could carry infantry grunts farther, over rougher terrain. The frame attached to the spine could support heavier loads of equipment. Mechanical arms could push or pull extreme weights.

I have to admit such esoteric matters as extending troop endurance and improving combat capability never mattered in my other life. The civilian one. Minus the boots and ABUs. It might not have mattered all that much to me now if DARPA hadn't insisted on a month-long orientation before exiling me to Fort Bliss.

Part of my familiarization program included a tour of the Soldiers' Support Center at Natick, Massachusetts. That was pretty interesting, actually. Those guys are doing some slick stuff. My orientation also included visits to several advanced research centers like MIT and Boeing's Skunk Works. The kicker, though, was a trip to Bethesda Medical Center, just north of D.C. While there I talked to men and women who might not have lost legs or arms or eyes if they'd been better equipped.

I'm not going to get schmaltzy on you, but . . . Well . . . Those interviews changed my perspective on a lot of things, this job included. I guess that's why I get that annoying feeling I told you about, the sense that I'm part of something important. I can't shake the hope my team might stumble across a new technology that could alleviate some of the pain and suffering I saw at Bethesda.

Even more irritating is the thought that sneaks into my head when I don't guard against it. If I stick out this assignment . . . If I complete my four years in uniform . . . Maybe, just maybe, I'll break the downward spiral that's been my life up to now.

Which is why I refused to let EEEK get the best of me. Determined to crack him, I scowled at the metal carcass. The skeletal creature smirked back. With some effort, I managed to suppress the notion that it was only waiting to get me in its clutches.

"Let's go over the power ratios one more time," I insisted. "I want to know precisely how much movement it takes to work the extremities."

NOT much, I discovered when I finally decided to climb aboard.

A simple on-off switch activated EEEK's built-in computers. Once he was powered up, I shed my tiger-stripe ABU blouse, tucked my dog tags inside my standard issue yucky brown T-shirt and folded myself into the metal frame.

Correction. It wasn't actually metal, but a feather-light composite that looked and felt like steel. The leg braces attached to my combat boots at heel and ankle. A springy tongue extended below each boot to air-cushion my steps. A web vest secured my spine to EEEK's. My hands slid through loops on the arm braces and into glove-like controls.

Encased in the frame, I felt a weird sort of reluctance to connect the headpiece and flip down the visor. I had the uneasy notion I was sublimating my brain to EEEK's. I couldn't escape the fact that his circuitry could process more data, more rapidly, with more accurate results, than mine.

I mean . . . Electronic "eyes" that register images in a continual, 360-degree sweep? Infrared sensors capable of identifying the heat signatures of everything from field mice to an incoming missile? A visor with more three-dimensional graphics than the latest version of Mortal Kombat? Gimme a break!

Most of it was off-the-shelf electronics available in games sold to pimply teens and perennial adolescents like my ex. What made EEEK truly innovative was that Harrison Robotics had combined the electronic circuitry and lightweight composite frame with an advanced ergonomic design that blended technology with robotic muscle.

"Minimize your movements," All Bent warned. "The gimbals respond to the slightest . . . Wait! Lieutenant! Don't lean forward like that!"

His frantic shout came too late. One slight bend at the waist and I was kissing the floor. It took the combined efforts of my entire team to haul me upright again. I swear to God I heard EEEK snickering.

"Minimize," the Harrison rep reiterated. "Just *think* about moving."

I got the hang of it. Eventually. Still, I spent a full day banging around the test facility, making sure I could interpret the data EEEK bombarded my visor with, before I ventured outside.

Bumping into walls and instrumentation stands was one thing. Dodging cacti and twisty-limbed mesquite was another. My first foray in the great outdoors left me cursing and the sadistic robot I was strapped into grinning from ear to composite ear.

Did I mention I'm a little stubborn? I hung in there. Not that I had much choice. The test parameters called for a twenty-mile run. In full combat gear. Carrying a sixty-pound pack. Someone—me, unfortunately—had to complete the run before FST-3 could write our field test report and stuff EEEK back in his crate.

I do know my limitations, however. No way I was ready to go full battle rattle for twenty miles. Not with the temperature hovering around 110 in the shade and the August sun so vicious that not even the scorpions would come out to play. Girding my loins—literally and figuratively—I managed two miles at a springy trot. The following day I upped it to five. Before I extended the distance much farther, I decided to test EEEK's low-light optics and terrain-following sensors.

I set the launch time for two A.M. My team of dedicated professionals protested vociferously, but I held firm.

The high desert cools off at night, you see. Not a whole lot this time of year, but enough to make the run semibearable.

So come two A.M. I encased myself in composite and took off. I headed south this time, toward the periphery of Fort Bliss's three-point-four zillion acres of test range. I sure as heck didn't want to head north. Although my team coordinated all its activities with the Fort Bliss Command Post, there was always the possibility those guys might forget to mention a little thing like a night firing exercise of a Patriot missile battery.

No missiles streaked through the star-studded sky. No explosions lit up the horizon, near or far. I moved slowly at first, getting a feel for EEEK's night vision capability. To my relief, he had eyes like a bat. His infrared imaging enhancement clearly illuminated hazards like clumps of spiny cholla and cracks in the hard-baked earth.

It also illuminated the odd-shaped hump ahead long before I picked up its stench. When the stink did hit, I figured I'd come across a dead coyote or mule deer. I was moving fast by then, too fast to swerve, so I decided to bound over the carcass and keep going.

Bad decision. Reeeeally bad.

I misjudged the distance in the dark and the springy foot pedal that gave EEEK its bounce caught on something, pitching me forward. Just in time, I threw my weight backward. The gimbals kept me upright, for which I'll be forever grateful. I don't even want to *think* what would have happened if they hadn't.

"What the hell . . . ?"

Gagging at the noxious stink, I lifted my visor to see

what had snagged my foot and found myself staring down into the bloated remnants of a face. It took me several stunned moments to realize a second corpse lay sprawled almost atop the first.

I was up to my ankles in putrefying human remains.

CHAPTER TWO

WHEN my traumatized brain kicked back into gear, I let loose with a screech loud enough to wake the dead. Not these dead, thank God. Decaying flesh spewed as I kicked free of the ribcage that had snared EEEK's foot pedal.

"OhGodohGodohGod!"

Shrieking, I lunged a good fifty or sixty yards before I thought to lower the visor and whip around to scan the darkness behind me. No ghostly figures had risen up from the desert floor to give chase. No poltergeists flew through the night air in my direction.

Still, I stumbled another dozen yards before I could bring myself to halt EEEK's forward momentum. Wrenching one hand free of the control glove, I grabbed frantically for the radio clipped to my belt.

"O'Reilly! Cassidy! Anyone! Come in!"

"Speak to me, oh Goddess of Gadgets." O'Reilly punctuated his reply with a jaw-cracking yawn. "Whazzup?"

"I just stumbled over some bodies."

"Huh?"

"Bodies." My voice rose perilously close to another shriek. "Like in *dead* people!"

"Jesus!"

I heard a loud thump that I guessed were his chair legs hitting the floor. The thud came nowhere near matching the volume of the hammering inside my ribcage.

"Call the county sheriff," I got out. "Give him my coordinates."

"Will do. Want us to come get you?"

Hell, yes, I wanted them to come get me! I had opened my mouth to order the entire team to pile onto ATVs when I remembered I was supposed to be a lean, mean fighting machine.

My notions of officership are still a little hazy around the edges but even I recognized that I wouldn't present a sterling example of a leader if I turned tail and ran—as I very much wanted to do.

"I'll stay at the scene until the sheriff arrives," I said with immense reluctance. "Just get him out here fast. And notify the Command Post at Fort Bliss of the situation," I added belatedly.

I wasn't sure who exercised investigative jurisdiction over putrefying remains on a remote patch of government range cut by two county roads. At this point, I didn't really care.

O'Reilly confirmed the coordinates transmitted by EEEK's built-in GPS and promised to get on the horn immediately. It didn't occur to me until after I'd signed off that whoever or whatever caused the death of these two people might still be in the vicinity. I grabbed the radio again, but common sense intervened.

Lord knows, I'm no expert on decomposition. My only previous experience with the dead was at my grandfather's funeral. In keeping with my family's long-standing tradition of loser-ship, Pop had passed out at the wheel of his semi after downing the better part of a bottle of Jack Daniel's. I was about four or five at the time, and my mother insisted I had to file past his coffin. I remember thinking Pop looked like Play-Doh.

These guys were way past Play-Doh. The desert sun had baked them to mush, so they must have been dead awhile. Or so I reasoned. Erroneously, I later found out. Seems searing heat speeds up the process of decomposition.

I didn't know that, however, and trusted my flawed logic enough to unstrap EEEK. He would require some cleaning when we got back to the test site. I would require several Valium. In the meantime I had nothing else to do but wait.

EEEK's presence proved oddly reassuring as the minutes ticked by. Moonlight glinted on his frame, and the faint beeping of his computer gave me the sense I wasn't out here with only two corpses for company.

I should tell you that even without the corpses, the desert gets darn spooky at night. Clouds moving across the moon throw eerie shadows on the baked earth. The saguaros and mesquite take on sinister forms.

Then there are the noises. The first time a burrowing

owl belted out its shrill, up-and-down warble, I almost wet myself. Moments later one of his buddies popped out of its hole and answered the call.

The thing about night sounds is that once you start listening for them, you hear them. All kinds of sounds. As if to challenge the owls, another songster piped up. It ran through a whole scale of notes, repeating them over and over until I was gritting my teeth.

I knew what it was. A western mockingbird. Despite a distinct lack of interest from the rest of the team, Pen—Dr. England—insisted on sharing her encyclopedic knowledge of the flora and fauna native to the north Chihuahuan Desert with us. I could hear her nasal whine in my head, droning away, almost as obnoxious as that mockingbird.

I was contemplating hurling a rock at the irritating warbler when a scuffling sound reminded me the night belonged to more than just birds. There was Pen's whine again, going on about gophers and kangaroo rats and sand foxes and—quick grimace here—hooded skunks, badgers, duck-billed bats, and Mexican gray wolves.

And coyotes. I couldn't mistake their distinctive yipping. The cries echoed well off in the distance at first but gradually moved in. With a sick feeling in the pit of my stomach, I remembered Pen's terse admonition not to leave any trash lying around at the test site as the scavengers will eat anything, dead or alive.

When an excited yip sounded in the vicinity of the bodies, bile spurted into my throat. I had to force myself to my feet and climb aboard EEEK so I could peer through his visor. An instant later, I wished I hadn't. Gagging, I yanked up my radio again.

"This is Spade. Where in blazes is the sheriff?"

"On his way," O'Reilly assured me. "May be a while yet, though. His vehicle isn't equipped with GPS. We're vectoring him to your location."

A shadow of movement sent another sour spurt into my throat. I swallowed convulsively. "What . . . ? What about the Fort Bliss Range Patrol?"

"Also on their way."

That left me, several owls, one mockingbird, the bodies and a pack of coyotes. I signed off again and debated my next move. No way I was getting between flesh-eating scavengers and their late night snack, but I couldn't just stand there.

After considerable internal debate, I picked up a rock and heaved. I'm no Dan Marino or Brett Favre. The missile thudded to earth well short of its target. Desperate now, I resorted to shouts and arm waving.

"Beat it! Scram! Shoo!"

It was the shoo that finally cleared the fog in my head. How stupid was that? How stupid was *I*? EEEK was designed to amplify and extend human extremities. I couldn't throw worth crap, but he could. Weighting my pockets with rocks, I strapped myself in, powered up, and let fly.

THE sheriff arrived just after dawn. His black-and-white raised a plume of dust a half mile long. I climbed atop a small rise to flag him down.

He wasn't alone. Accompanied by a deputy, he rolled out of the car, settled his straw Stetson low on his brow and squinted through the fast rising heat waves.

"Lieutenant Spade?"

"You were expecting maybe Madonna?"

The sheriff's brows straight-lined under the brim of his Stetson. His deputy's shot up.

Tough. I was in no mood for nice after hours spent chasing off coyotes.

"I'm Roy Alexander." The sheriff hooked a thumb at his sidekick. "This here is Tom Bartlett."

Sheriff Alexander was lean and rangy, with deep crevices carved in his weathered face. Bartlett was a younger version of his boss without the creases. Both men shifted their glances to the right.

"You want to tell me what that is?" Alexander drawled with another hook of his thumb.

"That is an Ergonomic Exoskeletal Extension."

"Come again?"

"My team tests inventions for the Department of Defense. This is one of them."

The curt reply had both sets of brows working again.

"Look, I'm tired and thirsty and totally creeped out." That was the closest I could get to an apology. "The bodies are over there."

The two law enforcement officials had obviously gone this route before. In what appeared to be a well-established routine, they extracted a jar of mentholated petroleum jelly from their vehicle and smeared a generous dollop across their upper lips, then each tied a handkerchief over their nose and mouth. Deputy Dawg retrieved a digital camera.

The sheriff pulled out a roll of plastic evidence bags. Both men snapped on latex gloves. Only then did they approach the bodies.

I stayed put.

Despite their precautions, the first good whiff made the sheriff gag. Deputy Dawg tossed up his cookies. The officers scrutinized the scene for a scant few moments before beating a hasty retreat.

"Critters been at 'em," the sheriff commented as he swiped his face with the handkerchief. "Bones and body parts are scattered all over the place."

I hesitated a moment or two before making a reluctant admission. "I might have had something to do with that. I was aboard the exoskeleton, testing its night vision capability and moving at a good clip. I slogged through the bones and, uh, stuff before I realized what it was."

Deputy Dawg scrunched his lips. I wasn't sure whether it was an expression of sympathy for a really unpleasant experience or exasperation that I'd messed up his crime scene.

"What about those rocks peppering the area?" the sheriff asked. "They your doing, too?"

"A pack of coyotes stopped by for a visit."

A hint of sympathy entered Alexander's eyes. "You've had quite a night, Lieutenant."

"And I'm feeling every minute of it."

"How about we get you some water and sit in the shade while you tell me the exact sequence of events?"

THE Fort Bliss Range Patrol arrived next. Two cops, one military and one civilian, both coated with dust from their long drive. The county coroner followed hard on their heels. His ambulance jounced over the rutted earth while I was rehashing my nocturnal activities to the Range Patrol.

The coroner and his assistant had come prepared. After conferring with the sheriff, the doc and his tech sprinkled liquid onto two surgical masks.

The masks must have proved more effective than mentholated jelly, as they waded right in. The rest of us watched from a safe distance while the tech did his thing and the doc wielded a pair of long-handled forceps.

"One of them has a wallet on him," he called out through his mask. "It has an ID in it. You want to examine it now, or wait till I finish?"

"Now," Alexander shouted back.

Nodding, the doc dropped the object into an evidence bag. His assistant delivered the bag to the sheriff, who examined the ID for all of ten seconds before letting out a long, low whistle.

"Take a look at this."

Deputy Dawg and the two Range Patrol officers crowded in. I peered over their shoulders but couldn't see what the excitement was all about.

"We'd better contact CBP," Alexander commented. "Pronto."

"Already done," the military cop replied. "Standard protocol these days. Mitch radioed to say he and another officer were ten minutes behind us."

You can't live or work along the Mexican border without knowing CBP stands for U.S. Customs and Border Patrol, formerly just the plain ole Border Patrol. They used to operate under the auspices of the Department of Justice but, like the Coast Guard and a bunch of other domestic agencies, got funneled into the huge bureaucracy known as the Department of Homeland Security after 9/11.

One of the CBP's unenviable tasks is to stem the tide of illegal immigrants—which is what I assumed the dead men were until this character Mitchell and his cohort drove up in a white 4x4 sporting the distinctive green stripe of the Border Patrol.

To say I disliked Agent Mitchell on sight would be a gross exaggeration. It took him a good three or four minutes to tick me off. The fact that he reminded me forcibly of my ex certainly didn't score him any brownie points. Same broad-shouldered build. Same muscled forearms showing under the rolled-up sleeves of his green utility uniform. Same long-legged stride.

The slender, dark-haired female with him also wore Border Patrol greenies. The assorted canisters, cuffs and weaponry attached to her belt must have weighed ten or fifteen pounds but she carried herself with the same self-assurance as this character Mitchell.

Only after he got closer did I make out the differences between him and Charlie. Mitchell had a square jaw that suggested a strength of character my ex had most definitely lacked. His floppy-brimmed boonie hat shaded eyes framed by squint lines carved deep in his tanned skin. I guessed the man had at least ten years on my ex, and a century of experience. Not all of it good, judging by those eyes.

They swept over me, lingered on EEEK for a few moments without registering a single emotion, then turned to his fellow law enforcement types.

"What have we got, Sheriff?"

"Two males. Sun baked 'em pretty good. They're nothing but buzzard bait now, Mitch. I'm guessing they've been dead fourteen, maybe sixteen hours. Doc Allen will give us a better fix."

So much for my theories on decomposition! I was counting backward fourteen hours, trying to figure out how close I'd come to finding these guys still alive, when Mitchell indicated me with a jerk of his chin.

"I take it she found 'em."

Not being particularly partial to chin jerks, I muscled in on their cop party.

"She did," I replied crisply. "Lieutenant Samantha Spade. I'm in charge of a DARPA test facility a few miles north of here. And you are?"

"Jeff Mitchell. This is Tess Garcia."

Agent Garcia treated me to a friendly smile. I started to return it when Mitchell nodded toward EEEK. "Is that what you were testing?"

"Yes."

"Alone?"

"Yes."

"At night?"

"Yes."

I had a good idea where this was going. Sure enough, Mitchell's mouth took a sardonic twist.

"Let me make sure I have this straight, Lieutenant. You went for a midnight stroll, alone, along one of the most permeable stretches of the U.S.-Mexico border. One highly favored by the scum who run drugs and human traffic across it nightly."

I could do the chin thing, too. Mine tilted at a sharp angle to match the acid in my response. "First, I was in constant communication with my base."

Not totally true. The radio had remained clipped to my belt for most of the run. Mitchell didn't need to know that, however.

"Second, I wasn't out for a stroll. I was conducting a controlled test of an expensive and highly sensitive piece of equipment."

Unfortunately Sheriff Alexander felt compelled to amplify on my reply. "Lieutenant Spade ran her equipment through the buzzard b—er, bodies."

"What?"

"Plowed right through 'em."

Mitchell and Garcia flashed me identical looks. On her, incredulous was okay. On him, it was not.

"She also kept the coyotes off," the sheriff added. "Or tried to."

That produced a sympathetic glance from Garcia and a grunt from her cohort.

"Before you check out the scene," the sheriff advised, "you might want to see this."

He handed over the bagged ID. Mitchell took one look at it and let out a long, slow hiss. Garcia's eyes widened.

"Holy shit! It's him!"

Once again I had to force my way into their cop circle. "Him who?"

Six pairs of eyes swung in my direction. Each pair

blazed with varying degrees of elation and fierce, almost feral, satisfaction. Agent Mitchell clued me in.

"The ID belongs to Sherman Brown, of Dennison, Texas. Brown reported it stolen a few weeks back, along with all his credit cards. We got a tip that someone attempted to use one of those stolen credit cards in Mexico two days ago. Someone matching the description of Patrick James Hooker."

The name sounded familiar. Enlightenment burst a moment later.

"The American mercenary?" I gasped. "The one suspected of selling the stolen arms used in that ambush down in Colombia last year?"

The ambush had made headlines. Six Colombians and three U.S. Marines moving in to raid a drug cartel's headquarters had died in a lethal crossfire. Hooker's role in the incident didn't come to light until he was captured in a similar raid some months later.

"That's him," Mitchell confirmed grimly. "Bastard was extradited to the U.S. and spent four months in pre-trial confinement before a judge ruled the U.S. government didn't have sufficient evidence to try him. He was being shipped back to Colombia for trial when he escaped."

Tess Garcia picked it up from there. Her delicate face had hardened into something almost ugly.

"We got a tip he intended to slip back into the States. Presumably to set up another arms deal. FBI, TSA, CBP and law enforcement officials from coast to coast have been on the watch for him."

"We didn't get him," Deputy Dawg said with profound regret, "but the desert did. Too bad the traitor wasn't still alive when the varmints started gnawing on him."

"He probably was."

That came from the coroner, who joined us just in time to catch the deputy's comment. Dragging down his mask, the doc addressed our startled group.

"Both men were shot. Can't tell much until I get them to the lab, but it looks like one got it through the back of his skull. Hooker took a hit in each kneecap, though. My guess is he lay there, baking in the sun, until he bled out or the ants and scorpions made a meal of him."

CHAPTER THREE

THE various law enforcement types surrounding me displayed little reaction to the coroner's grim pronouncement. I tasted hot and sour again.

Gulping, I felt compelled to mention at that point that bits and pieces of the deceased might be clinging to EEEK's frame. I stayed well away while the doc and his tech examined EEEK's lower extremities. They snapped some digital images, wielded their forceps once more, and returned with plastic evidence bags containing gobs of something I chose not to look at.

"It's been a long night," I said to Sheriff Alexander. "If you're done with me, how about a ride back to my test site?"

"Sure. Bartlett, help Lieutenant Spade load her . . . uh . . . equipment in the squad car."

"Hang on a sec."

Agent Mitchell's intervention earned a questioning look

from the sheriff and an irritated one from me. The sun had cranked up to full furnace by now. I was hot and tired and wanted to get out of my boots, baggy pants and sweat-drenched T-shirt.

"Talk to me about this thing." Mitchell eyed EEEK thoughtfully. "How does it work?"

"It's a robotic extension of the human frame. It uses computerized components and basic ergonomic principles to amplify the operator's capabilities. The composite frame supports up to a thousand pounds. The arms and legs extend both reach and endurance. The visor displays a spectrum of electronic signals."

"What kind of signals?"

I hooked a sweaty tendril behind my ear. "Speed, distance, terrain contouring, infrared heat signatures, to name just a few."

"So it sees in the dark?"

"Like a cat."

"How come it didn't see the bodies before you sashayed through them?"

"It did, but it displayed them as a lumpy mound. When I picked up the stench, I thought I'd come across a dead deer or coyote. I was moving too fast to swerve so I tried to jump over it."

Mitchell nodded absently. The composite frame held his interest more than my gymnastic shortcomings. Consequently, he missed the glare I was sending him.

"These electronic signals. Does the robot's computer store them?"

"Normally it would. For test purposes, however, we've bypassed the storage CPU. Now EEEK transmits directly to the computers back at our site so my guys could analyze the data real time."

"EEEK?"

Sighing, I repeated the litany. "Ergonomic Exoskeletal Extension. My team added the K for ease of reference."

"I see."

"Sheriff, about that ride . . . ?"

Once again, Mitchell intervened. "I'll drive you. I want to take a look at that data. Your robot's sensors may have picked something up."

"They did. A big lump of dead."

He scraped a palm across his bristly chin. The bristles were a dark gold that matched the flecks in his greenish eyes. Hazel, I guess you'd call them. I was wondering if the hair under his boonie hat was the same color as his whiskers when he terminated my contemplation of his person. Very effectively, I might add.

"If Hooker took a while to die," he commented, "odds are his killer hung around to watch."

I didn't particularly care for the idea I might have come close to rubbing elbows with someone who got his jollies by shooting people in the kneecaps and watching them writhe around in pain.

"I want to take a look at that data," Mitchell said again before turning to the sheriff. "Sorry to bail on you, Roy. I'll leave Garcia to run interference. Once word leaks that we may have found Hooker, every Fed in a five-state area is going to want a piece of the action. You'll have CIA, FBI and TSA agents coming out your ears."

"Yeah, I figured. No sweat. Let me know if that data turns up anything interesting."

"Will do. How do we get your friend here back to base, Lieutenant?"

I suppose I could have given him a demo of EEEK's ergonomic mobility, but there was no way I was climbing aboard until he'd been hosed down.

"Drive your vehicle over next to him and we'll load up."

My first inclination was to borrow a pair of the sheriff's latex gloves and shove EEEK into the 4x4's back compartment. In deference to all that expensive electronic circuitry, we ended up boosting him into the rear seat and belting him in.

THE ride back to CHU-ville was pretty bizarre.

EEEK lolled in the back seat of the Border Patrol Range Rover, looking very much like a cyborg out for a Sunday drive. I sat in the front with Agent Mitchell. Dust and hot wind blew in through the open windows, doing a number on my face and hair. We had to keep the windows down as EEEK had acquired a case of body odor, in the most literal sense of the word. The rush of hot air kept the smell at bay.

Mostly.

Yielding to the wind, Mitchell dragged off his hat and tossed it in the back seat beside EEEK. As I'd suspected, the dark oak of his hair matched the chin and cheek bristles. I also noted more than a few strands of silver mixed with the tawny gold and revised my estimate of his age. The man had at least fifteen years on Charlie.

"Tell me about your test unit." He pitched his voice

above the rush of hot Texas wind. "Are you part of TRA-DOC?"

TRADOC is milspeak for the army's Training and Doctrine Command. Fort Bliss is one of the command's largest installations. *The* largest, if you count its fifteen hundred square miles of unrestricted airspace in addition to its gazillion acres of range.

"We're a tenant on post," I informed him. "We're with the Defense Advanced Research Projects Agency."

"DARPA, huh?" He threw a glance in the rearview mirror. "That explains a lot."

I raised a brow in surprise. Our agency isn't all that well known outside DOD and academia. He caught my look and shrugged.

"I spent a few years in the navy, a long time ago."

"Can't be that long, Agent Mitchell. You don't look a day over fifty."

Actually I now had him pegged at a really buff thirty-five or six, but I owed him for that bit about traipsing through the desert. Alone. At night. Etc.

His lips twitching, he ignored the dig and extended an olive branch. "It's Mitch."

I felt compelled to offer the same courtesy. "And I'm Samantha."

"You don't go by Sam. Or Sammy?"

"Occasionally, when I feel the need to make folks think I'm one of the boys."

He aimed a quick look at me and the T-shirt stuck to my chest.

"Not much chance of that happening," Mitchell commented.

I was pretty sure that was a compliment but decided not to follow up on it. Since I was only peripherally interested in the lean, ropy muscles displayed by Agent Mitchell's rolled up sleeves, I shrugged aside his comment and filled him in on my cadre's mission. I should have filled him in on their personal idiosyncrasies.

The entire team piled out of the test facility when we drove up. I did the intros, and Mitch did some serious second looking.

I have to admit my crack professionals make a distinct impression. As is her habit, Pen had her salt-and-pepper hair screwed into a loose topknot and skewered with pencils. She didn't neigh when introduced, but came darn close. Brian "Rocky" Balboa fussed and fidgeted like a maiden aunt. O'Reilly squinted at Mitch through his Coke bottle lenses. Sergeant Cassidy, bless his macho soul, returned a handshake with the knuckle-crunch of Special Ops.

The prize went to the Harrison Robotics rep, though. All Bent tch-tched in dismay when he spotted EEEK propped in the back seat. "I hope you set the gimbals before you transported him this way!"

Not only did I not set the gimbals, I neglected to shut down his computers. I had started to inform All Bent of that when he yanked open the rear door.

"Ugh! What's that stink? And what is this?"

Before I could stop him, he swiped a finger over EEEK's foot pedal.

"It looks like . . . Oh, God! Is this . . . ? Is this . . . ?"

"'Fraid so."

His face went dead white. His eyes rolled back in his

head. Next thing I knew, his three hundred plus pounds were stretched out at my feet.

IT took a while to get down to business after that somewhat inauspicious start. Plus, I refused point blank to review or release any data until I'd showered and changed into a clean uniform.

Mitchell was waiting with a cup of the herbal tea Pen badgered us all into drinking instead of coffee. His expression was so carefully neutral that I had to laugh.

"Gawdawful, isn't it?"

He glanced around, saw Pen wasn't within earshot, and grinned. "And then some."

Whoa! Someone should tell the man to smile more often. That simple rearrangement of facial features softened the hard line of his jaw and crinkled the squint lines at the corners of his eyes.

Charlie! Remember Charlie!

It was my personal call to arms. My own version of Remember the Alamo. I chanted it whenever I needed a reminder of the last time I let my hormones get the better of me. I repeated the mantra again, dragged in a deep breath and assembled my team.

"Agent Mitchell wants to . . ."

"Mitch," he corrected.

There it was again. That crooked grin. Dammit all to hell.

Charlie! Charlie! Charlie!

"Mitch," I informed my team, "wants to review the signals and imagery EEEK transmitted last night."

Our software guru, O'Reilly, whistled through his teeth. "We're talking twenty or thirty million gigabytes. It'll take all day to download it."

"Even longer to interpret," Rocky added. "Our data synthesizer employs a simplified digital filter with sigma-delta quantized tap coefficients," he explained earnestly, "but it's a simple off-chip loop filter."

Mitchell looked at me. I looked at the ceiling.

"I'm only interested in sequences captured immediately before and after Lieutenant Spade's encounter with the victims."

O'Reilly's frown evaporated. "No problemo. I know just where to look. I inserted a marker when she radioed in, screaming about how she'd tripped over some dead bodies."

"I may have been a tad excited," I conceded, "but I didn't scream."

"Ha!"

O'Reilly snorted, Cassidy huffed, Rocky twitched, and Pen let loose with a high-pitched neigh that caused Mitchell to blink and hunch his shoulders.

"You screeched like a '69 Impala in urgent need of a ring job," O'Reilly announced. "My ears still hurt."

"About that data . . ." I said pointedly.

Thus adjured, my team got to work. Even with the marker, however, it took hours to download and synthesize the data EEEK had transmitted.

We then listened to an electronic chorus that included the owls, the mockingbird, the yipping coyotes, a squeaky cry that sounded like kil-dee, kil-dee. Pen identified it as emanating from a Killdeer. That's a bird, she informed me when I looked at her blankly. I didn't ask how a bird could kill a deer. I'd had enough gore for one night.

We also listened to me. I won't bore you with a repeat of my transmissions right after I stumbled across the victims. I've already admitted those weren't my finest moments.

Although . . .

A couple of my more colorful expletives did produce another grin from Mitch. This one was so wicked I completely forgot my ex's name.

I remembered it right about the time Mitchell's cell phone pinged. He flipped it open and identified himself. I thought I recognized the feminine voice on the other end as belonging to Agent Garcia.

My guess proved correct when Mitchell hunched his shoulder to anchor the phone. Digging into his pocket, he produced a pen and notepad.

"Okay, Tess, shoot."

He didn't like what he heard. His speckled green eyes grew stormy and his jaw went all square.

"Where and when?" he barked. "Yeah, yeah, I'll be there. Just hold the fort."

The cell phone flipped shut. Mitchell stuffed the pad and pen back in his pocket and threw me a disgusted look.

"That was Agent Garcia. Agents from the El Paso FBI office and Fort Bliss's CID detachment are converging on the scene as we speak. They want to compare notes with Sheriff Alexander and me. We're meeting at Pancho's."

Pancho, whose full name remains a mystery, runs a bar/cafe/motel/convenience store in Dry Springs. The only bar, cafe, motel or convenience store in Dry Springs.

Some folks claim Pancho lost the sight in his left eye in a free-for-all following a Mexico City soccer match. Others insist his wife jammed a thumb in the socket after catching him with a younger woman. Wish I'd thought of that. However he'd acquired it, Pancho's black eye patch and his bar were fixtures in this corner of West Texas.

Frowning, Mitchell checked his watch. "This could take a while. The FBI is bringing in its own forensics team. I want to see what they turn up. I'll call you and let you know when I can get back down to the site."

"How about I call *you* when we finish analyzing the data? If we find anything, I can run the results up to Dry Springs."

"That'll work." He scribbled his cell phone number on a notebook page, added Agent Garcia's for backup and tore out the sheet. "I'll make sure one of us is available when and if you call."

WE struck pay dirt late that afternoon. Literally and figuratively.

It didn't look like much at first. A blurred digital image recorded in that instant before I whipped up my visor to see what the hell had snagged EEEK's foot pedal. The bodies showed only as greenish lumps, which was fine with me, but Rocky got all twitchy. That's his way of expressing excitement. That, and an unfortunate tendency to expel gas.

"We can re-synthesize this," he exclaimed. "I'll lighten it to show more detail. Might be something here Mitch can use."

I didn't stick around to watch. I'd already gotten up close and personal with the Gruesome Twosome. I had no desire to repeat the experience. Instead I went into our admin center and used my laptop to Google one Patrick J. Hooker.

Even with the tabloids' usual 99.9999999% margin of error, Patrick J. Hooker was one bad dude. A native of Michigan, he'd joined the army at eighteen and shipped out right to Iraq. Didn't take him long to realize the hired guns working for private contractors like Blackwater and Kellogg Brown & Root made mega-bucks compared to the average grunt.

After his time in uniform, Hooker returned to Iraq as a mercenary but was hustled out of the country after an incident involving a young Iraqi girl. He popped up next in Colombia, where he *allegedly* brokered a deal with a big-time drug lord for a shipment of stolen arms. A joint U.S.-Colombian Drug Eradication Task Force went in to recover the arms and were ambushed en route. The ensuing shoot-out left three U.S. Marines and six Colombian police officers dead.

I say allegedly because despite Hooker's extradition to the States and long months in pre-trial confinement, prosecutors couldn't prove he was the one who actually delivered the stolen arms. His lawyer subsequently pushed a writ of habeas corpus through the courts and the U.S. government was forced to dismiss all charges for lack of direct evidence. The Colombian government took it from there and were transporting Hooker back to their country for trial when he escaped.

I was skimming through an article summarizing the

complex legal issues in Hooker's case when a shout summoned me back to the lab.

"Lieutenant! Take a look at this."

"This" was a boot print almost hidden by the bodies, which Rocky had synthesized to nauseating clarity. The print was etched in blood and showed the tread pattern in startling detail.

"You stepped right on it," Rock said. "The next sequence shows EEEK's pedal coming down, then scrabbling around before it sprang up and left only a smudge in the sand."

I remembered that sequence. All too well.

"Make me several copies of the print. I'll take them to Agent Mitchell."

I stuffed the copies in a manila envelope and left with a final admonition to my team.

"EEEK's still outside. Get All Bent to help you clean him up and bed him down for the night."

I slammed the door on their instant chorus of protests.

CHAPTER FOUR

THE dirt parking lot at Pancho's normally sports three or four dusty pickups with dented cattle guards and the occasional bullet hole in the rear window.

When I chugged up to the sprawling adobe establishment just past six P.M. in my beat-up Bronco, an assortment of government vehicles crowded the pickups. Jeff Mitchell's 4x4 with the Border Patrol's eye-popping green stripe was parked alongside Sheriff Alexander's patrol car. The Fort Bliss Range Patrol was there, as well as several unmarked sedans with government license plates.

I crammed on my patrol hat and snuck a peek in the rearview mirror. *Not* to check my lip gloss before sauntering in to join the boys. I'd already applied a coating of Georgia Peach one-handed a mile back. I just needed to make sure my hair didn't straggle down and—God forbid!—touch my collar. That infraction of the sacred rules could earn me a firing squad at dawn. Or worse, assignment to ice-bound FST-1.

Grabbing the manila folder containing copies of the digitized boot print, I made for the bar/cafe entrance and plunged from searing sunlight into the perpetual gloom of Pancho's.

It's the kind of place that bombards your senses the instant you walk in. Stale cigarette smoke vied with simmering green chili stew to assault the olfactory nerves. Ropes of fly-specked neon and an astonishing collection of *Sports Illustrated* bathing suit–issue covers make your eyeballs spin. Kenny Rogers and Sheena Easton were belting out a classic on the radio. You don't want to know what I felt crunching under the soles of my boots.

"*Hola*, Lieutenant." Pancho peered through the gloom with his one good eye. His handlebar mustache lifted into a grin. "Heard you had some fun last night."

"Only if you have a really twisted idea of fun."

Planting both palms on the bar, I levered up and delivered the kiss on cheek Pancho expected from all regular female customers under the age of ninety. I dropped back on my heels with the sweet, vanilla taste of Father's Moustache Wax on my lips.

Pancho often declared to anyone who would listen— and several of us who tried very hard to shut him out— that Father's was his favorite brand. I'd looked it up once on the Internet. The wax promised to make any mustache stand up, lay down, roll over, or play dead. Pancho's fell into the last category.

"You here to join the pow-wow?" he asked, nodding to

the back room euphemistically referred to by everyone in Dry Springs as City Hall.

In fact the room *did* host meetings of the town council. Such as it was. Also a Saturday night poker game that had gone on for as long as anyone could remember.

When I replied in the affirmative, Pancho said he'd bring my usual to the table. I started to shake my head and inform him I was still more or less on duty. But his reminder of my "fun" night made something a little stronger than a soft drink seem not only desirable, but absolutely imperative.

With the promise of imminent liquid stimulation, I made my way to City Hall. I could tell by the handwritten notes and reports scattered across the table they'd been hard at it. There were crime scene photos, too. All of which a scrawny guy in jeans and severely wrinkled cotton shirt covered up as I approached. He slammed his notebook shut, too, which kinda torqued me off.

Weren't we all supposed to be operating in a more enlightened age, with government bureaucracies cooperating in the common goal of kicking the baddies' butts? Scrawny Guy obviously hadn't received the memo.

Tess Garcia smiled a welcome while Agent Mitchell made the intros. "This is Lieutenant Samantha Spade. She found the vics."

I nodded to Sheriff Alexander and the civilian from the Fort Bliss Range Patrol.

"Andrew Hurst," Scrawny Guy supplied tersely. "CID."

For the uninformed, CID is the army's Criminal Investigation Division. Counterpart to the air force's Office of

Special Investigations and the navy's Naval Criminal Investigative Service.

I know the official names, but until now most of my knowledge of military investigations came from watching that John Travolta movie about the kinky general's daughter. The rest I've absorbed while drooling over Hot Buns Mark Harmon in the NCIS TV series.

This guy Hurst was no Mark Harmon. Rail thin and intense, with eight or nine strands of straw-colored hair stretched across his otherwise bald pate, he wouldn't qualify for hunk status in anyone's book. I immediately changed his moniker from Scrawny Guy to Comb-Over while Mitch introduced the next member of the conclave.

"Paul Donati. El Paso region FBI."

Also very trim, but sporting dark, Italian eyes and a full head of wavy black hair. I felt a stir of interest, immediately squelched when I noted his wedding band.

I shook his hand and hid a grimace when he did the finger-crunch thing. Why some guys feel compelled to exert their masculinity by grinding your bones is one of the mysteries of the universe, right up there with summer sandals hitting department stores in January and winter boots showing up in July.

Not that I've bought many boots lately. You wouldn't, either, if you had to clump around fourteen hours a day in government issue clod hoppers. These suckers come off, my flip-flops go on. Winter, summer, whenever.

But I digress. Back to our conclave. I retrieved my hand from Donati just as Pancho appeared with my shot of tequila and another round of beer for the others at the table. Except for tough, macho Agent Mitchell, that is. Pancho placed a dew-streaked can of Diet Dr Pepper in front of him.

I cast back to my days as a ruffled-pantied cocktail waitress at the Paris Casino in Vegas. I was trying to remember if I'd ever served someone with ropy muscles like Agent Mitchell's a diet anything when he sent a pointed glance at the manila envelope I'd placed on the scarred tabletop.

"What have you got for us?"

Ha! Like I was going to show my stuff after Comb-Over slammed his notebook in my face?

I let them all wait while I took a lick of salt, slammed back my shot and bit into the lime wedge. The tart, tangy combination jolted through my entire system and went a long way toward compensating for a night spent with coyotes and decaying bodies.

"You first," I countered when the jolt subsided. "Tell me what you've found out since you left the test site."

Mitchell lifted a brow at my arbitrary command but complied. "We ID'ed the second set of remains."

"How?" I didn't really want to know but curiosity got the better of me. "There couldn't have been enough of him left to run his prints. Unless the guy was carrying an ID . . ."

"He was carrying several, all fake. But he'd very obligingly marked himself in law enforcement data systems worldwide by tattooing his right ass cheek. The coroner was able to piece together enough skin for us to run him through NCIC and IDENT-IAFIS."

"Ident-a-face?" I smirked. "Apropos, wouldn't you say?"

"IDENT-I-A-F-I-S," Mitchell spelled out with exaggerated patience. "The tattoo popped for one Juan Sandoval. He had outstanding warrants for one count each of armed robbery, aggravated assault and attempted murder, with three counts of transporting illegal aliens into the U.S."

"Nice guy."

"Almost as nice as his traveling companion."

I certainly agreed with that after Googling up Dead Guy Number One.

"We also got a preliminary report on the bullets. Appears they were M118LRs, chambered in a 7.62mm."

"Translation?"

"They're special rounds manufactured primarily for military sharpshooters. The markings on one round indicate they might be part of a batch purchased for use by USMC snipers. We won't know for sure until we get the final ballistic report."

Uh-oh! I'm not usually real good at connecting the dots but these were too big and fat even for me to miss. Three U.S. Marines dead in the shoot-out down in Colombia. The prime suspect in that ambush killed by a marine sniper bullet. Hard to stretch that into mere coincidence.

"There's a USMC detachment at Fort Bliss," Comb-Over put in. "They conduct surface-to-air missile training for navy and marine personnel. Stingers and Avengers."

I fidgeted a little in my chair but didn't say anything. No need to advertise the fact that I'd enjoyed a *really* intense weekend with one of the instructors at the Surface-to-Air Weapons Officer Course. The captain and I parted company soon afterward but the memories lingered—right up until I was jerked back into the present by Mitch's low murmur.

"The snipers of the sky."

I shot him a curious look. Was he remembering his navy days? Had he been trained to fire one of those shoulder-held Stingers?

Seeming to retreat inside himself for a moment, he dropped his glance to his Dr Pepper can. My glance followed his down and lingered on his hand. It was strong and weathered like the rest of him. It was also ringless.

That didn't mean squat, of course. Lots of married men don't wear wedding rings. My jerk of an ex, for example. Still, it said a lot for my state of my mind after a close encounter with persons of the dead variety that I hadn't paid much attention to Agent Mitchell's bare left hand until this moment.

"I'll contact the lieutenant colonel who commands the marine detachment," Comb-Over said as he angled away from me and wedged his notebook open a minuscule three or four inches to make a note.

Geesh! This was getting ridiculous. You'd think I was sporting a hammer and sickle on my uniform instead of a subdued, desert-toned Velcro patch that identified me as one of the Good Guys.

For a moment or two I seriously contemplated handing over the manila envelope with the copies of the digitized boot print and retiring to the bar and Pancho's more genial company. I might have done just that if I hadn't caught Mitch's eye-roll and Sheriff Alexander's barely smothered grunt. The fact that they didn't like this smarmy little CID jerk, either, kept me in place.

When I did present the print, everyone went nuts over its clarity. So much so that both the FBI and CID wanted full access to all data downloaded from EEEK.

I wasn't precisely sure about Harrison Robotics's proprietary rights or DARPA's policy vis-à-vis handing over test data but I was kinda out-gunned here. I resorted to a stall to give me time to discuss the matter with All Bent and my supervisor.

"My guys are processing the data as we speak. We're talking hundreds of millions of gigabytes. I'll make it available as soon as it's downloaded."

When the cop party broke up a short time later, I decided on one more shot of tequila. I took it at the bar and ordered a bowl of Pancho's green chili stew as a chaser.

Now, don't go all preachy and judgmental on me. I know my limit. I won't tell you what it is, but suffice it to say that with a family history like mine it's a sure bet I don't overindulge in hard liquor. Right now, though, I wasn't particularly eager to head back to CHU-ville and another night punctuated by Pen's equine whistles.

I was nursing the tequila when the two Border Patrol agents delayed their departure to join me at the bar for a few moments. I'd already had a taste of Jeff Mitchell's bluntness. Still, the look he lasered in my direction caught me as unprepared as his question.

"What do you know about the Marine Corps detachment on Fort Bliss?"

"The detachment? Nada."

Interesting how many emotions an elevated eyebrow can convey. Particularly when it hikes up over a penetrating, cut-the-crap stare.

"I saw your reaction when the subject came up."

"What reaction?"

"You squirreled on your chair like someone just hauled into hard secondary for questioning."

Hard secondary being the containment area at border crossings where suspicious characters are taken for further questioning. Having made several jaunts across the Rio Grande to sample the ubiquitous delights of Juárez, I'm a little surprised I have yet to visit the holding pen. I've seen a few folks hauled off, though, and squirrel they did.

"What was that about, Samantha?"

"Nothing subversive," I said with a nonchalant shrug. "I went out with one of instructors from the school a few months back."

Agent Mitchell, it turned out, was more interested in my connections than my currently nonexistent love life. "You've got an in at the school? Someone who might talk to you?" he persisted, those gold-green eyes drilling into me.

"Well . . ."

"Call him. Set up a meeting asap."

Now, I'm only a brown bar. That's second lieutenant, in civilian speak. Just about every commissioned officer in every branch of the military outranks me. Including, I was surprised to learn, the uniformed officers of the Coast Guard, the Public Health Service and the National Ocean-ographic and Atmospheric Administration.

I've heard of the Coast Guard, of course, and know the PHS runs the Indian Clinic in El Paso. Don't quiz me on NOAA, though. I think they're hurricane hunters or space cadets or something.

The point I'm laboring to make here is that the U.S. Border Patrol is *nowhere* in my chain of command. Even if it was, I've already confessed I haven't completely mastered the art of taking orders. So of course I bristled and came within a breath of telling Agent Mitchell to go take a flying leap. He spiked my guns with a terse addendum.

"Make the meeting off-post."

I deflated like the NASDAQ after another sharp spike in crude oil prices.

"Why off-post? And why," I wanted to know, "the end run around Mr. Comb-Over?"

"Who?"

I jerked my chin toward the now empty back room. "Special Agent Hurst."

Tess Garcia smothered a sound suspiciously close to a chuckle. Mitchell merely shrugged.

"I've worked with Andy Hurst before. Or tried to. He tends to view inter-governmental cooperation as a one-way street."

"Yeah, I got that impression."

I nursed my grudge against Hurst and his notebook until Mitchell abandoned Tess and me for the men's room. Swinging around on my barstool, I followed his progress.

I'll say this for the man. He exhibits all the personality of a warthog at times but he does have one fine butt. When I swung back around, Tess Garcia was watching me with speculative eyes.

"What?" I asked, feigning an air of innocence that wouldn't fool a five-year-old, much less a highly trained and heavily armed Border Patrol agent.

She tapped an unpolished fingernail against her beer

bottle, obviously weighing how much to share with an outsider. I was about to check my uniform for a hammer and sickle again when she finally responded.

"You want to be careful there. Mitch hit a rough patch a few years ago. He's still working his way back."

I've seen what rough patches can do to folks. Particularly the dysfunctional whiners and winos I call family. I was giving Agent Mitchell credit for dragging himself out of whatever pit he'd fallen into when I flipped up my cell phone and scrolled through the contacts.

I'd thought about deleting USMC Captain Danny Jordan from my call list after our one weekend together. He's hot. *Extremely* hot. But he's way too gung ho for a non-lifer like me. I mean, he has his skivies laundered and pressed!

Yo! This is Dan Jordan. Leave a message. Beeeeeeeep.

"Dan-O, this is Samantha Spade. I need to talk to you. Give me a call when you get this . . ."

"Heya, Sweet Cheeks. Long time no see."

Or speak. Or touch. Or swallow each other's tongues.

"What's up?"

"Can you break away tomorrow? I'd like to talk to you."

A wary note crept into his voice. "What about?"

I'd heard that tone before. From my ex, when I wanted to discuss our relationship.

"It's not about us," I informed him.

"Good to know." His relief was palpable, which says a lot about Dan the Man. "So what's this about?"

"I'll tell you tomorrow. How about lunch? Twelve o'clock at the Smokehouse."

"Can do. See you then."

I flipped the cell phone shut just as Mitchell returned.

"We're set," I informed him. "Noon tomorrow, at the Smokehouse."

"Good. Pick me up at the Ysleta Border Patrol Station. Eleven-thirty."

"You know," I said with some feeling, "it might be nice if you *asked* sometime instead of just dictating."

A look of genuine confusion crossed his face. He glanced at Tess, who offered only a bland smile. The light dawned eventually, and he repeated the order/request with exaggerated politeness.

"Pick me up at the Ysleta Station. Eleven-thirty. Please."

I gave him my most brilliant smile. "Will do."

Blithely unaware I had just put the lives of my entire team on the line, I settled in to enjoy my green chili stew and shoot the breeze with Pancho.

CHAPTER FIVE

I drove back to the test site with the late August twilight coming on fast. The Franklin Mountains were a jagged purple smudge in the distance. Night-blooming cacti were getting ready to burst into showy white blossoms on either side of the two-lane road.

By this time of day, most of the roadkill had been either flattened or picked clean by buzzards so I didn't have to dodge too many bloated armadillos. I kept a wary eye out for mule deer, though. I'd missed one by a twitch of his tail a few months back.

When I arrived at the site, the temperature had plummeted from a sole-searing one hundred eight to ninety-six or seven. My internal thermometer rocketed up again, however, when I saw EEEK still outside, pretty much where he'd been unloaded this morning.

Scowling, I marched to the only CHU with lights showing. A blast of refrigerated air hit me when I opened the door to our D-fac. 'Scuse me. That's dining facility, which in this case includes a microwave, a coffeemaker, a fridge, a table and four chairs. Crowded into the other half of the CHU was a sofa, a couple of chairs and a TV with a satellite dish. Oh, yeah, and the Universal Gym.

Sergeant Cassidy was on the bench, clanking away. Pen had her shoulders hunched and earbuds stuffed in her ears while she listened to yet another incomprehensible treatise on supernovas or the mating habits of blowfish or something.

Brian Balboa and Dennis O'Reilly sat at the table, the remains of a microwaved pizza between them and their laptops open. Rocky, I didn't doubt, was studying the specs on the next item we were supposed to test. Our little twitch of an engineer is as dedicated as he is gaseous. O'Reilly was deep into a computer chess match. I saw an animated knight put a king in check and shut the door with an irritated thud.

"Hey, guys. What's the idea of leaving EEEK out where the gophers can nibble on his circuitry?"

O'Reilly kept his eyes glued to his laptop screen. Cassidy clanked away. Pen hadn't even heard me come in. It was left to Rocky to explain.

"We discussed the matter and everyone agreed. Scraping human remains off test equipment isn't included in our job descriptions."

"It's not in mine, either." I huffed, although my scant months as a team leader had taught me that argument was totally bogus. Being in charge has its perks, most of which

I've yet to experience. It also has a definite downside. Whatever idiot coined the cliché about the buck stopping here obviously never worked with my team.

"Where's All Bent?" I asked in a desperate attempt to fob EEEK off on the Harrison Robotics rep.

"He packed up and left right after you took off for Dry Springs."

I guess I should have expected that. The man had hit the ground like a dead buffalo.

Still . . .

"Benson reminded us that DARPA assumed full responsibility for EEEK when you signed for him," O'Reilly put in without looking up from his chess match. "He's your baby until you complete the required tests, oh Queen of Quack Inventors."

I knew that.

Still . . .

I resorted to bribery and offered comp time for any civilian who volunteered for clean-up duty. When that pathetic stratagem didn't work, I fell back on the old stand-by of whining. My team remained unmoved.

That's the thing about working with highly educated civilians. They know their rights, darn it.

Heaving a long-suffering sigh, I pulled rank on the only other military member of FST-3. Sergeant Cassidy at least was obligated by law to follow the orders of the officers appointed over him.

"Noel! Front and center!"

I tried to bark the command like a crusty old veteran but it came out sounding cranky and petulant even to me.

"My psychiatrist isn't gonna like this," he grumbled as he disengaged from the steel cage of the gym.

Cassidy's delicate mental state was the least of my concerns at the moment. I was more worried about EEEK's residual stink.

"We'll need something to block the smell."

While I glanced around the CHU, Cassidy solved the problem for himself by dragging off his sweat-soaked T-shirt and draping it around the lower half of his face.

I was too grossed out to admire the body-builder torso thus revealed. Although it did make me wonder if your own sweat smelled as rank to you as it did to everyone else. Something to ask Pen about, I decided. Later.

I retreated to the CHU I shared with her to fashion my own face mask out of a T-shirt liberally laced with Chanel No. 5.

I'd splurged on the perfume in a moment of sheer madness. I could have trotted across the border and bought a cheap imitation but, no, I had to hit the Post Exchange and shell out mega-bucks for the real thing. Sucker that I am, I actually believed the woman at the counter when she quoted Marilyn Monroe's famous line. The one where MM claimed all she wore to bed was two drops of Chanel No. 5. I figured what the heck. If it worked for her . . .

Wish I could tell you it worked for me. The few times I've squirted on the stuff out here in West Texas, all I've attracted is swarms of gnats.

A few bugs were infinitely preferable to EEEK's eau de corpse, however. Tying on the makeshift mask, I grabbed my toothbrush and the spray bottle of disinfectant Pen insisted on washing our sink and toilet with twice a day. Pure spite made me grab *her* toothbrush as well.

Sergeant Cassidy and I regrouped outside the lab and went to work. We made quite a pair. Two trained warriors on our knees in the dirt, our faces muffled by perfume-and-sweat soaked T-shirts, cleaning an expensive piece of equipment with toothbrushes by the light of the moon and a strategically positioned Super Brite.

Happy I was not. For this I had turned in my ruffled panties? For this I'd abandoned the bright lights and big tippers in Vegas?

Noel wasn't any more pleased with his demotion from Special Ops to toothbrush wielder. He alternated between glowering at me, at EEEK, at me again.

Our foul mood lightened a little when Rocky broke down and joined us. He'd swathed his entire head in a bath towel. Peering through a narrow slit in the folds, he knelt beside Noel. I sent a silent prayer winging heavenward that he wouldn't add to our discomfort by cutting loose with one of his world-class bloopers.

Guilt or shame or the end of his chess match brought O'Reilly out a few moments later. Our resident nerd wasn't about to pick up a toothbrush but he did condescend to hold the high-beam flashlight at a better angle.

Pen was the last to emerge. Tugging off her ear buds, she scanned the scene with a puzzled expression.

"What's going on?"

"They're digging for clams," O'Reilly drawled.

Sarcasm bounces off Dr. Penelope England like bullets off Superman's chest.

"Don't be ridiculous. Bivalve mollusks haven't inhabited this region since the Permian-Triassic period more than two hundred and fifty million years ago."

Tch-tching, she poked around in her lopsided bun for a pointy object and joined our little work party.

I was feeling marginally more charitable toward my team when we finished with EEEK. Despite our meticulous scrubdown, though, he was still too ripe for the lab.

After much discussion we decided to tuck him back in his shipping container and stash him in the storage shed where we usually parked our ATVs. As I screwed down the lid I could swear I detected a look on his computerized face that promised dire retribution for the day's indignities.

WE made the news the next morning. Not me personally. My two dead acquaintances.

I was identified only as a "military officer conducting tests on an isolated section of Fort Bliss's range." That kind of miffed me. You'd think I would have earned at least a few seconds of notoriety.

I got over my snit real fast, though, when one news spot showed Sheriff Alexander with about a hundred microphones shoved in his face. He answered several queries in his laconic West Texas drawl but let Paul Donati speak for the FBI and do most of the talking.

The big story was Patrick Hooker, of course. His remains had been positively ID'ed using dental records, although back-up DNA testing was in the works. The media coverage cut between his shell-shocked parents in Michigan and the sleazoid attorney who'd sprung Hooker from pre-trial confinement.

Naturally the lawyer claimed his client had never brokered stolen arms, much less been present at the shoot-out where U.S. and Colombian troops died. Neither the FBI nor Sheriff Alexander would release the exact details of Hooker's demise, saying only that the investigation was still ongoing.

I watched the coverage for a while, checked on EEEK in his container and decided to leave him in situ while my team downloaded the rest of his data.

They were still hard at it when I drove into El Paso for my meeting with Mitch and Danny Jordan. I dressed up for the occasion in a fresh set of ABUs. Nothing like boots, baggy pants and a blouse with more flaps than a 747 to make a girl feel really special.

My first stop was the Ysleta Border Patrol Station. The station is a cluster of buildings in what used to be a primarily agricultural area that had gotten caught up in El Paso's urban sprawl. The fenced yard was large enough to house a fleet of vehicles, most of which were out on patrol at the moment. The yard also contained a maintenance depot and a nondescript administrative building where the agents stood muster prior to going on shift.

The Border Patrol's primary mission used to be to deter illegals and smugglers. After 9/11, priority shifted to apprehending terrorists attempting to enter the U.S. Hence Mitch's direct involvement in the Patrick Hooker case. That much I knew.

What I didn't know was the staggering statistics that smacked me in the face after I showed my ID and was asked to wait in the reception area.

A Hot Sheet pinned to the bulletin board indicated that on a typical day, Customs and Border Patrol personnel process some 1.13 million passengers and pedestrians entering the U.S.; 70,000 truck, rail and sea containers; and $88 million in fees, duties and tariffs. They also apprehend 2,400 folks and seize more than 7,000 pounds of narcotics. *Daily!*

I was multiplying 7,000 by 365 in my head and not liking the result when Mitch appeared. He was also in uniform but his bristled with its usual twenty pounds of communications and weapons gear. Despite the assorted weaponry, he looked darned good.

Warning sirens went off in my head and I launched into my mantra.

Charlie! Charlie! Charlie!

"Sorry you had to wait."

The chant wasn't working so I gave it up and returned his smile. "No problem."

"I was going to give you the two-dollar tour. Maybe when we come back."

"Sounds good."

We walked out to my twelve-year-old Bronco, which earned a disbelieving grunt from Agent Mitchell. Brow cocked, he conducted a walk-around.

"What did you do? Drive off the side of a cliff?"

"Only about a third of those dents are mine," I informed him loftily as we strapped in. "The rest come compliments of my ex. So does the Bronco, for that matter. I traded my semi-new Mazda for this pile of junk and a quickie divorce."

Despite my bad-mouthing, the Bronc turned over with barely a wheeze. Mitch waited until we cleared the gate to the parking lot to pick up on my last comment.

"How long were you married?"

"Six months, twelve days, four hours." I turned onto the on ramp for I-10, thought about his ringless left hand and took a shot. "You?"

"A little longer." His boot slammed the floorboard. "Jesus! Watch the truck."

"I got it."

I wedged in behind a new-car transport rumbling over from the GM plant in Juárez with a good seven or eight inches to spare.

"How much longer?" I asked, curious.

"Thirteen years, give or take a few months."

He didn't amplify and I didn't press, although I suspected the demise of a thirteen-year marriage might have something to do with the rough patch Tess Garcia had mentioned.

Interstate 10 curved north, and we cruised toward the high-rises of downtown El Paso. Framed against the backdrop of the Franklin Mountains, their glass walls shimmered gold and coppery in the sun.

"We ran the boot print," Mitch said, frowning as I whizzed past a string of slower moving vehicles. "It's from a size nine-and-a-half medium Justin Rancher with a dual density EVA outsole."

I'd spent enough time in Texas to recognize the brand, if not the EVA stuff. As the name implied, it was the boot of choice of working ranchers in the area.

"The tread was fairly new so the FBI is canvassing retail outlets in a tristate area."

"How do rancher boots fit with military sniper rounds?" I wanted to know.

"Good question. I'm hoping your marine friend might suggest an answer."

We took the exit for Highway 54 and headed north. The high-rises quickly gave way to apartments and residential areas. A few miles on, the family neighborhoods yielded to the bars, strip joints and tattoo parlors found within close vicinity to military installations worldwide.

The Smokehouse was considered safe in that no one had been knifed there in recent memory. Although it wasn't much more than a hole-in-the-wall, the restaurant was at least three or four rungs up the couth ladder from Pancho's. Its walls weren't plastered with pictures of swimsuit models, and the only things that crunched under my boots as I wove a path through the jammed tables were peanut shells. I hope.

What made the place so popular was that its menu consisted of barbeque, barbeque, and more barbeque. You could get it sliced, shredded, pulled or still on the rib, all served with heaping sides of slaw, fries and slow-simmered beans. But that's all you could get.

Since the owner had done a hitch in the Corps and proudly displayed the eagle, globe and anchor above the cash register, his place was usually crammed with marines from the detachment at Bliss. Those of us wearing the uniform of other branches of the service were lucky to get a foot in the door.

Danny had arrived early and was fighting off his pals to hold a table. I wove my way through the jumble of boots and uniforms in his direction.

"You're looking good, Dan-O."

And then some! In fact, he looked almost as good as the first time we'd met, when his razor blue eyes and quicksilver grin had drawn me like a moth to the proverbial flame.

The grin came out again, making me question why I'd let his gung ho personality douse the fire.

"Back at you, Sweet Cheeks."

His glance cut to Mitch, noting the Border Patrol patch and the holstered Heckler & Koch on his hip. I made the intros, they did the hand crunch thing, and we all went to the counter to place our orders. The Smokehouse's amenities don't run to a waitstaff.

"So what's this about?" Dan asked when we'd taken our numbers and carried our soft drinks back to the table.

"Putrefying flesh."

"Huh?"

"I ran into some out on the Fort Bliss range. Maybe you saw the news coverage this morning?"

"That was you? The 'unidentified military officer'?"

His sympathy for my traumatic experience lasted only a second or two. Then he recalled the identity of one of the corpses and his blue eyes went flat and cold.

"The news stories didn't say what went down out there. Hope to hell Hooker took a long time to die."

I left it to Mitch to reply.

"Long enough." He leaned forward and engaged the captain eye-to-eye. "The FBI lab is working the ballistics, but it looks like someone pumped specially chambered M118LRs into both victims."

Danny grasped the significance of those rounds instantly. "You think a marine sniper took the bastard down?"

"I think it's a possibility."

"If so, we should pin a medal on the shooter. Hooker smuggled the weapons that killed good men."

"Unfortunately, that had yet to be proven."

Dan's upper lip curled. "Because he got sprung on a technicality. If I was Hooker's attorney, I'd be checking my six."

Checking six being the military's polite way of saying the sleazy lawyer better watch his ass. Mitch ignored the editorial.

"Got any marine snipers assigned to your school, Captain Jordan?"

"None that fire anything smaller than a Stinger missile."

"You sure about that?"

"I know every one of the instructors."

"How about the students? How many are going through the schoolhouse at present?"

Dan sat back in his chair, his eyes narrowing. "Is this an official inquiry, Agent Mitchell?"

"Yes."

"Why here?" He paused and let the noisy conversations and rattle of cutlery underscore his question. "Why not on post, at the school?"

"Various law enforcement agencies will contact your detachment commander, if they haven't already. When Lieutenant Spade mentioned she had an in at the school, I figured I'd cut right to her source."

Dan didn't appear to appreciate being tagged as a source and shot me an unfriendly look.

"Hey, I'm not real happy about all this, either," I protested. "My team and I were up half the night cleaning human remains off a sensitive piece of equipment. We've also put our test schedule on hold to process data gathered at the scene, which means we'll be stuck out in Dry Springs for longer than anticipated. You ever been to Dry Springs, Dan-O?"

Mitch overrode my mostly rhetorical question and zeroed in on the tight-jawed marine. "How many students currently in training?"

"Thirty-eight. Twenty-nine in the Stinger Gunner/Avenger Crew Member class, nine going through Surface-to-Air Weapons Officer training."

"You have access to their duty history. I need to know if any of them ever trained as a sniper or served in the same unit with the men killed in the Colombian shoot-out."

Dan wanted to tell him to take a flying leap. The signs were subtle but I picked up on them. His bulldog chin went square. His blue eyes turned arctic.

"Someone knew Hooker intended to try to get back into the U.S.," Mitch said quietly. "When, where, how. They were waiting for him and took him out. That's murder any way you cut it."

He let that sink in for a few seconds before continuing.

"Whatever you and I may think of Hooker's actions and ultimate demise, Captain, I've sworn to uphold the law and you to protect and defend the Constitution of the United States. No one in this country, not even Patrick Hooker, deserves a self-appointed firing squad."

Wow! That was some heavy stuff. I was feeling the weight of the Constitution on my shoulders when Dan-O scraped back his chair and dug out his wallet.

"I'll clear your request with my CO and provide whatever information he deems releasable." He dropped some bills on the table. "Now if you'll excuse me, I think I'd better skip lunch and get back to the school."

Mitch and I watched him thread through the crowd, shoulders rigid, chin jutting. More than one pair of eyes cut from the captain to us.

"That went well," I commented dryly. "Think he'll come through with the requested information?"

"Yeah." Mitch's gaze followed the stiff-necked marine. "He knows I can go over his head and get it from Headquarters. Better for the school to cooperate and, if necessary, work damage control with the local authorities."

MITCH and I departed the Smokehouse two shredded beef sandwiches and a pile of grease-soaked fries later.

I drove him back to the Ysleta station and he gave me the promised two-dollar tour. The yard was buzzing with agents coming off shift and others preparing for the afternoon muster.

Tess Garcia lifted a brow when she spotted Mitch doing tour guide duty and gave me a friendly wave. The warning she'd issued at Pancho's kicked around in the back of my mind as I gained a distinctly sobering insight into a border patrol agent's typical duty day. And I thought I had it rough out there in the desert!

After promising to keep Mitch posted on the EEEK data dump, I rattled off in my Bronc. The promise had nothing to do with any desire to see Agent Mitchell again. Okay, maybe a little.

First, though, I needed to check with my boss at DARPA about proprietary rights and release of said data. Turning over a re-synthesized boot print to federal authorities was one matter. Releasing everything else EEEK's computerized brain had ingested was another.

I spent most of the afternoon in the air-conditioned comfort of my office on Fort Bliss. After checking in with my team and confirming they were hard at it, my first task was to compose and zing off a detailed email to my boss. I could have called, but he spends most of his day in meetings and I wasn't in the mood for an extended game of telephone tag.

I also took the time to skim through several new test proposals that had landed in my in-box while I was out in Dry Springs, communing with snakes and scorpions. One looked really interesting. Non-line-of-sight goggles that supposedly would let the wearer see around corners, over obstacles and through walls. I got caught up in the specs and spent some time trying to decipher them.

I hit the Post Exchange and Commissary before leaving Fort Bliss. Thinking to reward my team for their reluctant cooperation last night—and ensure their future cooperation without having to resort to begging, pleading or whining—I stocked up on frozen pizzas for Rocky and Pro-Sport Multivitamins with high oxygen radical absorbance capacity (whatever that was!) for Sergeant Cassidy. O'Reilly got the latest issue of *Chess Moves*. Pen a Nature's Rhythms CD featuring a collection of whale songs.

Since I was in town, I also decided to swing by my apartment and check my mail. That led to an extended session in my very own shower, which I actually had room to turn around in. I followed that unparalleled luxury with a quick wash/tumble dry of my ABUs.

Consequently it was dark when I finally headed back to Dry Springs and almost midnight when I turned off on the spur that led to our site. I was humming along with Travis Tritt when I spotted the flashing red lights in my rearview mirror. Cursing, I glanced at the speedometer and saw I was only going twenty miles over the limit. Hardly worth worrying about out here in Nowhere Land.

Still cursing, I slowed down and pulled over. Moments later, the Dry Springs Volunteer Fire Department's only pumper roared by. The wash made my Bronco shimmy and rattle like an old tin cup.

I got a weird feeling as I watched the fire engine zoom over a small rise. It looked like it was headed straight for my site.

I shoved the Bronco into gear, stomped on the gas pedal and dug in my breast pocket for my cell phone. I was stabbing frantically at the speed dial button when I topped the rise and spotted the red glow lighting the night sky.

CHAPTER SIX

I reached O'Reilly after three frantic tries and shrieked into my cell phone.

"*Dennis!* What's going on?"

"The lab's on fire!"

"No one's in there, are they!"

"No."

His reply shoved my heart back down my throat and into my chest.

"What about the lab's W-K unit?" I asked when I could breathe again. "Did it kick on?"

"Don't know."

With all our expensive test equipment, the CHUs we used as a lab had been rigged with a waterless fire suppression system that was supposed to be kind to the environment as well as our computers and electronic media. We'd never had occasion to test it before.

"Gotta go," O'Reilly gasped, sounding close to hyper-ventilation. "The fire truck just pulled up."

"I'm right behind it."

Mere moments later I brought the Bronc to a screeching halt a safe distance from the pumper. I scrambled out, my horrified gaze on the flames leaping from the lab. Obviously, our handy-dandy, environmentally friendly fire suppression system had failed its first test.

While the DSFD volunteers un-snaked their hoses with Sergeant Cassidy's able assistance, I raced over to the rest of my huddled squad. Pen was in the faded Stanford University T-shirt she wore to sleep in. Poor Rocky was shaking and twitching almost uncontrollably. Dennis's frizzy hair stood straight up. Below that orange crown, he was naked except for his black-rimmed glasses and a pair of boxers. I'd never seen his pudgy, milk-white torso before and sincerely hoped I never would again.

"How did it start?"

"No idea." He shoved his glasses up on the bridge of his nose with a forefinger. "Rock and I had hit the sack. Pen, too. Noel was still working out. He's the one who spotted the flames and sounded the alarm."

We all jumped as an arc of water slammed into the metal-sided CHU. With sledgehammer force, it shattered the unit's one window. To vent the flames, I learned later. At the moment, though, it was all I could do not to groan at the thought of the expensive equipment inside getting doused.

While we watched, stunned, another emergency vehicle came careening down the spur road, its lights flashing and siren screaming. The siren cut off and the black-and-white pulled up a moment later. A tall, lanky individual in jeans and a tan shirt with one tail hanging out emerged. As he crammed on his straw Stetson, I recognized Deputy Dawg from our previous meeting.

"Lieutenant."

I couldn't remember his name so I acknowledged his greeting with a nod. His gaze skimmed over my companions, widening a little when it hit O'Reilly before returning to me.

"Everyone accounted for?"

"Yes."

His relief was patently obvious. Apparently Deputy Dawg didn't like getting up close and personal with corpses any more than I did.

It seemed like an hour but was probably only about ten or fifteen minutes until the DSFD doused the leaping flames and the fire sizzled out. I was staring in dismay at the blackened exterior shell of our lab when one of the volunteer firefighters approached. He pushed his helmet to the back of his head and squinted at me with his one good eye.

Did I mention that in addition to running the only commercial establishment in Dry Springs, Pancho also serves as its mayor and a volunteer firefighter? If not, forgive me. It's been an eventful few days.

"We'll go inside shortly to check for hot spots," Pancho informed me.

Sweat poured down his face and dripped from the ends of his mustache. A hot August night is a real fun time to rig out in full protective gear.

"We notified the Fort Bliss Command Post when we got

the 911 call. They have a unit on the way. Want us to poke around to see if we can determine how the fire started or wait for them?"

Geesh! Shows you my state of mind. I hadn't even considered jurisdictional issues until this moment.

"Poke away."

He and one of his cohorts donned self-contained breathing apparatuses. To protect against toxic fumes that often resulted from electrical fires, I was informed. Switching on high-intensity search lights, they disappeared inside the lab.

At that point I rallied my troops and mounted a belated raid on the fridge in the D-fac. We returned with bottles of water and a carton of cherry Popsicles from Pen's private stash for the sweat-drenched volunteers. They carried their own re-hydrating supplies inside the pumper but seemed to appreciate the Popsicles.

Engine #5 from the Fort Bliss range protection fire station arrived while Pancho and his buddy were still inside the lab. I identified myself to Assistant Chief Rodriguez and his crew, then one of the Dry Springs guys gave him a situational assessment. That basically boiled down to:

"The fire's out and we still don't know the cause."

Nodding, Rodriguez instructed his crew to stand down. Helmets and and self-contained breathing apparatus went back in the unit. Fire retardant turn-out coats came off.

When the team stripped down to boots, pants and T-shirts, I couldn't help noting that, unlike the Dry Springs volunteers, these pros were almost as buff as Sergeant Cassidy. I was admiring the tableau they presented when Pancho stuck his head out the door. He'd removed his mask, so I had to assume the air inside the lab hadn't registered any toxicity.

"Lieutenant! You wanna come see this?"

I didn't. Not really. I knew I'd have to fill out reams of reports regarding damage to government property and dreaded what I might find inside. Consequently, my feet dragged all the way to the front door.

My first, joyous impression was that the interior didn't look all that bad. Then Pancho swung his high-intensity beam in a slow arc and burst my bubble.

Water seeped from the scorched ceiling in silvery ropes and splattered onto the blobs of melted metal and plastic that used to be our computers. Our racks of test equipment hadn't fared much better.

"Look's like the fire ignited over there."

My heart sinking, I followed the beam to Brian Balboa's pride and joy. The mega-expensive data synthesizer would never gobble up gigabytes again.

"Could have been a short," Pancho mused. "Or . . ."

"Or?"

"I dunno."

He scrunched his lips and shifted them from side to side. His bushy black mustache went along for the ride.

"The scorch pattern looks off to me. We'll have to wait until morning for a more accurate assessment, but I'm thinking the guys from Fort Bliss may want to send out their arson investigation team."

"Arson!"

I'm ashamed to admit it now, but the first thing that jumped into my head was a composite portrait of my team. Every member of FST-3, me included, had expressed a desire to nuke, firebomb or otherwise obliterate our forward operating location at least once. Some of us more than once.

Hard on that thought came another. FST-3 had evaluated and rejected some really off-the-wall inventions. One that leapt instantly to mind was a body spray that was supposed to absorb the sun's rays and convert them to energy pulses. After the spray raised blisters on my face and arms the size of moon craters, I'd sent a certain high school chemistry teacher what might be categorized as a slightly unprofessional rejection letter. He'd reacted with a hysterical phone call that concluded with the crash of glass beakers being hurled against walls.

There were others. I was composing a whole list of bitterly disappointed inventors in my head when I abandoned the lab and accompanied Pancho to consult with Assistant Chief Rodriguez.

NEEDLESS to say, FST-3 didn't get much sleep that night. The third night in a row, I might point out.

Pen insisted on brewing herbal tea to soothe our frayed nerves. Thankfully, she abandoned the rest of us for bed around two-thirty A.M. Rocky, Dennis, Noel and I immediately dumped the tea and brewed a pot of coffee so strong I was sure it would put hairs on my chest.

Now I don't want to give the impression we were nervous about this arson business. However, Sergeant Cassidy *did* remove the weight selector shaft from the Universal Gym. His jaw working, he whapped the rigid pole against his palm a few times before announcing that he was going out to patrol our site perimeter.

That left me slugging back coal-tar coffee and debating whether I should shut down operations or put in a priority requisition for a sidearm.

Lest you think the latter another of my more hare-brained notions, I should tell you that I qualified at the expert level on the military standard issue 9mm Beretta at Officer Training School. I guess I should also mention that was one of the *few* portions of the curriculum I excelled at. Doesn't matter. The idea of strapping on a 9mm semiautomatic was very appealing at that moment.

It was close to four A.M. when I retired to the CHU I shared with Pen. Her snuffles and snorts combined with the 180-proof caffeine kept me wide awake until dawn. As a consequence I was not quite at my best when the Fort Bliss arson investigation unit arrived.

The fact that CID Agent Andrew Hurst, aka Comb-Over, accompanied the team didn't exactly improve my mood. I knew military arson investigations crossed functional lines. Specially trained firefighters provide the thermal expertise. Criminal Investigation Division agents add their input on the criminal end. I also knew the Fort Bliss CID detachment was as strapped for manpower as every other unit in the U.S. Armed Forces, with more than half their personnel deployed to Iraq or Afghanistan. That didn't mean I appreciated being treated like a suspect by Comb-Over.

"You weren't here at the time of the fire, Lieutenant Spade?"

He had his pen poised and his notebook open. Angled away so I couldn't see his scribbled notes, of course.

"I was in El Paso. I arrived back on-site the same time as the pumper from Dry Springs."

"Mind telling me what you were doing in El Paso?"

"I met Agent Mitchell for lunch, worked some paperwork at my office, hit the PX and Commissary, then stopped by my apartment to check my mail."

I'm not sure why I didn't mention the meeting with Captain Dan Jordan. Must have been the way Comb-Over crabbed his shoulders to block my view while he jotted my response in his notebook.

"What time did you arrive at your apartment, Lieutenant?"

"I'm not sure. Six P.M. Maybe six-thirty."

"And you left when?"

"Around eleven."

"You needed four hours to check your mail?"

"I also took a shower and washed my uniforms. Why? What difference does it make *when* I left El Paso?"

"I'm just trying to establish a timeline."

Like hell. There was something going on here. Something I didn't understand but was starting to feel goosey about. I got a clue what it was when the CID agent treated me to a very unfriendly look.

"I spoke to the lieutenant colonel who commands the USMC detachment on post yesterday afternoon. He informed me you and Agent Mitchell have decided to conduct your own investigation into the death of Patrick Hooker."

Ooops.

"Not so," I countered without much hope of convincing

my interrogator. "Mitch simply wanted to talk to a friend of mine."

"Talk, or request sensitive information outside official CID channels?"

I wasn't letting him draw me into that quagmire. "You have problems with Agent Mitchell's actions, you take them up with him. In the meantime, how about you find out what made my lab light up the sky?"

THAT was my last exchange with Agent Hurst until he approached me several hours later with the lead arson investigator in tow.

My team was with me. We'd been standing around outside the lab, ignoring the early morning heat and wondering what, if anything, the investigators might uncover.

We found out when the lead investigator displayed a plastic evidence bag containing two intertwined scraps of wire. Their red plastic coating was almost entirely burnt away but enough remained for our resident test engineer to frown at the twisted strands.

"Where did these come from?" Rock asked. "We don't use wire with that type jacketing in any of our test instrumentation."

"Are you sure?"

Rocky drew himself up as much as five foot, seven inches of skinny PhD can.

"Yes, I'm sure. This coating is polychloroprene. It's used primarily on wire exposed to rough usage, oils, chemicals or other harsh solvents. None of which we expose our sensitive instrumentation to."

The lead investigator hefted the evidence bag in the palm of his hand. He was a young Robert De Niro type, dark-haired and dark-eyed, with a mouth that looked like it wanted to smile but couldn't quite get there.

"We found these strands attached to the circuitry controlling the lab's H-K system. Appears someone disabled the feed from the sensors."

"Sunnuvabitch!" That spewed out of me, not Rock. "So that's why the system didn't activate!"

Hurst gave me a look that said my outburst didn't eliminate me from his list of suspicious characters. Young De Niro merely nodded.

"Arsonists tend to have favorite methodologies," he said slowly. "I read a case study a few months back about one whose signature includes using polychloroprene-coated wire to short circuit electrical fire suppression systems."

Whew! That let my team off the hook. I was almost certain none of them were serial arsonists. Now all we had to consider was a whole list of disgruntled inventors . . . until the investigator's next remark knocked them off the radar screen, too.

"We suspect this guy is some kind of a rogue agent, as he seems to have insider knowledge and hits mostly high-profile government targets."

FST-3? High profile?

My team emitted sounds that ranged from Pen's neigh to a collection of disbelieving grunts.

"Whoever hit your lab," the investigator concluded, "his primary objective appears to be your data retrieval systems and synthesizer. It sustained the most direct damage."

I finally grasped the implications of the investigator's comment. It hadn't occurred to me until this very moment that the arson might be linked to the data EEEK gathered the night of Patrick Hooker's murder.

Data I'd promised to provide to an assortment of government agencies. *Much* higher profile government agencies than FST-3.

THE arson investigation unit continued sifting through the mess in the lab, so my team and I retreated to the air-conditioned comfort of the D-fac to assess our losses as best we could.

Dennis used his laptop to pull up our equipment inventory while Pen and Rock worked up a status report on the tests we'd completed prior to the fire and those that had been pending.

There was only one, thank God. Small stuff compared to EEEK. Who, I should add, was still nestled in his coffin in our storage shed.

The initial estimate of our losses made me swallow. Several times. List in hand, I put in a call to my boss and got his voice mail.

"Dr. J, this is Lieutenant Spade. I'm with my team onsite. We, uh, have a problem. Please give me a call."

I was still waiting for him to return my call in midafternoon. The delay gave me time to refine my list. Unfortunately, it also gave me time to reflect on my role in this latest disaster.

I kept thinking about Special Agent Hurst's timeline questions. Could a four- or five-hour detour to my apartment to clean up and wash a few uniforms be construed as AWOL or desertion? I didn't see how, as I'd made the stop after normal duty hours. Except the lines between on- and off-duty tend to blur when we're out here in Dry Springs.

I seemed to recall reading something about abandoning your post under fire being punishable by death. I was confident that meant enemy fire, not the kind you toast marshmallows by. Just in case, I was about to power up my laptop and peruse—you guessed it!—the Uniform Code of Military Justice when my cell phone pinged.

I took a deep breath and glanced at the number displayed on Caller ID. The air whooshed out of my lungs again. The area code was El Paso, not the hallowed "571" of DARPA's headquarters in Arlington, Virginia.

"Lieutenant Spade."

"It's Mitch, Samantha."

Charlie! Charlie! Charlie!

No use. The sound of his deep-timbered voice sent a shiver down my spine.

"Heard you had a problem out there last night."

"Yeah, we did. Who told you about it?"

"Sheriff Alexander. He says there's talk of arson."

"We're past the talking stage. I have a team of investigators on-site right now. They've found evidence that someone deliberately short-circuited the lab's fire suppression system."

Mitch chewed that over in silence for a second or two.

"No one was hurt, were they?"

"Not in the fire, but we're all kinda shaken. Rocky—Dr. Balboa—especially. He's in deep mourning for his sigma-delta quantized whatevers."

"Come again?"

"His data synthesizer took a direct hit. Everything we downloaded from EEEK was vaporized."

"Not everything," Mitch reminded me. "You produced the boot print. There's something breaking on that print, by the way."

"What?"

"The FBI's running that show. I don't have the details."

"Give me a call when you do."

"You got it."

He signed off, and I went back to Googling up the UCMJ.

CHAPTER SEVEN

WHEN my boss finally returned my call, I was fairly confident I wouldn't face a firing squad for deserting my troops under fire. It was almost five o'clock our time, six P.M. in Virginia. It was also, I remembered belatedly, Friday evening.

Normally my team would have shut down operations and been driving back to El Paso about this time. Or, if we hadn't completed our on-site evaluation, been heading to Pancho's for a little R&R before tackling the remainder of our tests on Saturday morning.

No R&R tonight. Sergeant Cassidy had already declared his intention of patrolling the perimeter again while Rock, Pen and Dennis searched for salvageable items in the lab and I refined the initial damage estimate.

I had some preliminary figures ready when my boss

called. Dragging in a deep breath, I hit the talk button on my cell phone.

"Lieutenant Spade."

"Hi, Lieutenant."

That light, mellifluous voice didn't belong to my supervisor, but rather his executive assistant.

"This is Audra. Dr. Jessup would like you to switch to video conference mode. Let me know when you're set and I'll put him on."

I swallowed a groan. My hair had long ago escaped its clip and straggled down my nape. I'd draped my ABU blouse over the back of my chair and was wearing only my sweat-stained brown T-shirt and dog tags. Worse, I hadn't even *thought* about lip gloss since the arson investigation team had arrived at the crack of dawn.

"Hang on a sec, Audra."

I scrambled into my blouse and twisted my hair off my neck. No time for gloss, though. As ready as I could be, I hit the video net switch on my cell phone.

I think I mentioned that DARPA is all about gee-whiz technologies. My DARPA-special cell phone is a prime example. It combines the latest in encryption technology with satellite communications and really cool graphics. The thing could probably receive signals from the Hubbell Space Telescope if I figured out the right commands.

Unfortunately, it also displays my boss's face with startlingly vivid, three-dimensional clarity. One glimpse of his pained expression told me he'd already heard about our lab meltdown.

Deciding to brazen it out, I gave him a smile and a chirpy, "Afternoon, sir."

"Good afternoon, Samantha. I heard you had a fire at the site last night. Not from you, I might mention."

I didn't bother to ask how he knew. Obviously the incident had warped across the government ionosphere with the speed of Hans Solo in his younger years.

"Yes, sir, we did."

"Why don't you give me your version of the events?"

I wasn't surprised he would assume my version might differ from whatever he'd heard. It usually did. At least he was willing to listen to my side of things. That's more than could be said for my previous bosses.

When it comes right down to it, I like Dr. David Jessup. I also respect him tremendously. He's one of those brilliant, freewheeling thinkers DARPA brings in for a five- or six-year stint to shake things up and go after the really far-out technologies. His mind-boggling list of credentials includes more degrees than you can count, a fellowship in Harvard's prestigious Science, Technology and Public Policy Program and two terms as president of the National Institutes of Health's Black Scientists Association.

All this at the ripe old age of forty-two. Although I have to say his fuddy-duddy bow tie and houndstooth check sport coat make him look years older. Maybe that was the point.

The problem is, Dr. Jessup's exposure to the military is as minimal as mine. We arrived at DAPRA the same week, which was probably why he got stuck with being my boss. Poor guy didn't know enough to run for cover.

After all our months together, Dr. J still isn't quite sure where a lowly lieutenant holding only a bachelor's degree fits into an organization composed almost exclusively of PhDs. I'm still not sure, either, but I don't let it keep me awake at night.

I did, however, need to give him the details of what *had* kept me awake last night.

"I wasn't here when the fire started, sir. I had a meeting with the Border Patrol regarding the bodies I discovered out on the range. Then I went to my office to do a little work. Did you get the email I sent you yesterday regarding the issue of proprietary rights?"

I inserted that bit about going to the office deliberately. I know I said I was almost certain I couldn't be accused of desertion but it never hurts to build your case.

Thus reminded that I was on post and diligently at work yesterday, Dr. J nodded. "I read it."

"I spotted the flames when I drove back out to the site later that evening. They pretty much consumed the CHU containing our test instrumentation."

Dr. J winced. I understood why with his next comment.

"You'll have to fill out a report."

The military loves reports almost as much as acronyms. Even DARPA, long considered a maverick among Department of Defense agencies, is not immune. You could paper Beijing's Bird's Nest Stadium with our required reports. Kind of ironic when you consider the billions we pour into research for non-written, non-verbal forms of communications.

"My team and I are already working it," I assured the good doc. "I'll get it to you Monday morning."

He looked relieved until I added a kicker.

"You may want to check DOD Directive 7200.11 concerning damage to government property. Once you receive my report, you or someone above you in the DARPA chain of command has three days to appoint an investigating officer."

That had to be a first!

Me, citing a government regulation!

My palms got clammy and I experienced a momentary faintness at the thought I might have gone over to the dark side. I gulped and recovered enough to continue.

"We had an arson investigation team out here for most of the day. They said it'll take at least a week for lab tests to confirm their findings, but they're 99.9 percent sure the fire was deliberately set."

"Any indications who might have set it, or why?"

I thought about mentioning my list of disgruntled inventors but stuck to the facts, such as they were.

"The lead investigator thinks he spotted a signature element. He says the arsonist may be a pro. A rogue agent who targets high-profile government agencies."

Dr. J went fish-eyed. "FST-3? High profile?"

I decided not to mention I'd had exactly the same reaction.

"I'm only telling you what the investigator said, sir. In any case, the fire settled the question of proprietary rights. Every bit of data we extracted from Harrison Robotics's Ergonomic Exoskeletal Extension went up with the lab."

"What about the exoskeleton itself?" he asked, obviously worried about another report, this time for the loss of expensive private sector property assigned to the government for testing. Neither of us wanted to *think* about the paperwork that might generate.

"We had it stored in a safe location. It didn't sustain any damage."

"And the other evaluations FST-3 had scheduled?"

"We'd completed all but one. The remaining item we intended to test hadn't arrived on-site yet, so we're okay there."

I hesitated a few seconds before broaching the sensitive issue of money. DARPA pours millions into research that could prove vital to the military's war-fighting capabilities. That's its sole purpose in life. But after 9/11 the huge cost of conducting the war on terror had done a number on DARPA's internal operating budget, as it had on every other government agency's.

"If we're to continue on-site testing, we'll need to replace both the CHU and our equipment."

"Yes, well . . ." Dr. J cleared his throat and tried to look supervisor-ish. "Send me your report and I'll check into funding for replacements."

"Yes, sir."

I hung up and spent the next few moments waffling between the nasty wish he wouldn't come up with the funding and the reluctant hope that he would. It was that damned inner conflict again. The one where I really, really wanted out of the responsibilities that came with my uniform but . . .

I spent the rest of the evening struggling with the loss/damage report while my team continued to sift through the remains of our lab. If you've ever had occasion to deal with the Department of Defense, you'll know why my jaw soon settled into a permanent lock.

DOD Directive 7200.11 referred me to DOD Regulation 7000.14. This is a multi-volume tome that provides how-to instructions for everything from requesting reimbursement for a missed meal to lobbying Congress for a new supersonic space transport.

The how-to's I needed were embodied in Volume Twelve, Chapter Seven. This sported the daunting title of *Financial Liability for Government Property Lost, Damaged or Destroyed*. The word "liability" sent up an immediate red flag. So did the paragraphs dealing with negligence, willful misconduct and unauthorized use of said property.

And I thought the Uniform Code of Military Justice was scary!

Wondering if it was too late to a) resign my commission and scuttle back to Vegas or b) purchase several million dollars in personal liability insurance, I plowed through Chapter Seven. I had to remind myself repeatedly that my task was simply to submit the initial loss/damage report. Once Dr. J appointed an inquiry officer, he would answer the required follow-on questions. Like . . .

Would a reasonable and prudent individual have acted in this manner?

What were the circumstances that existed when the loss occurred?

Was the individual on the job when the loss occurred?

I almost choked over "reasonable and prudent." As far as I knew, no one had *ever* hung either label on me. The bit about being on the job didn't do much for my nerves, either. I had to hope that brief detour to my apartment didn't come back to bite me.

My eyes were blurred and my head aching when I finally called it quits for the night. As I exited the D-fac and headed for the mini-trailer I shared with Pen, I spotted Sergeant Cassidy's brawny form silhouetted against a fat, round moon.

I paused, totally exhausted but suddenly feeling guilty. A program analyst doesn't get a lot of experience in mounting a perimeter defense. Yet even I recognized one man couldn't do it alone.

Feet dragging, I crossed the hard-baked earth. Sergeant Cassidy spun around, steel rod at the ready.

"It's me, Noel."

"We should establish an IFF signal," he said as I approached. "We need to identify friend or foe without giving away our position."

I searched my tired mind and came up with a suggestion.

"We've still got EEEK. We could uncrate him, power him up and put him on alert. God knows, he can see and hear in the dark better than either one of us."

"Good thinking, Lieutenant. Let's get him out of his box. Then you need to hit the rack," he said with a hint of gruffness. "You've had a pretty rough time of it the past few nights."

"So have you."

"I snatched a power nap this afternoon."

"That's not enough to last you through an all-night stint on patrol."

"Not to worry. O'Reilly and I worked out a rotation schedule."

My jaw dropped. Our pudgy, nearsighted software guru pulling guard duty? With only the night critters and EEEK for company? The mind boggled.

I could come up with only one rationale for O'Reilly's unnatural act. He no doubt figured—as did I—that the arsonist had accomplished his objective last night and wouldn't make a return visit. Nevertheless, I insisted on taking the four-to-six A.M. shift.

So EEEK and I greeted another dawn together. I kept Sergeant Cassidy's weight rod and my radio in hand while EEEK's computers bleeped quietly in concert with a chorus of desert night sounds.

WITH the morning light, FST-3 prepared to pack up and depart CHU-ville.

We'd established a routine over the months the team had been together. Using individual checklists, we divided our labor and made quick work of shutting down the site. The damage to the lab altered the sequence somewhat, but we got everything done.

Rocky, Pen and I loaded the equipment we thought might be salvageable into our team's van. Dennis emptied the fridge in the D-fac, bundled up our trash and hauled all disposables to the Dumpster. Noel shut down power to the CHUs, then drove the ATVs into the storage shed. The spare gasoline cans went into the back of his pickup to be refilled for our next deployment to Dry Springs.

Whenever that might be.

Our last act was to padlock the storage shed and CHUs. Although no lock would keep out anyone who wanted into the charred lab, I didn't want to be accused of not properly safeguarding its barbecued remains.

Our personal gear, briefcases and laptops filled the remaining space in our vehicles to near capacity. Dennis rode with Noel in his truck. Pen and Rocky took the loaded van.

That left my trusty old Bronc as the only means of transporting EEEK. I wasn't about to strap him into a passenger seat, as Mitch and I had after my close encounter with the dead guys. I could just imagine the double takes and wheel jerks if I cruised I-10 with a grinning cyborg beside me.

Instead, we left him in his crate and slid him into the back of my Bronc. I made a mental note to contact Harrison Robotics to advise them of EEEK's status as I stopped by Pancho's to tell him we'd shut down.

"I'll drive by the site once in a while to check on things," he promised, as he always did.

"Thanks."

"Want a cool one before you hit the road?"

I was tempted but shook my head and leaned over the bar to give him a kiss on the cheek. All I craved after the past few days was the quiet, messy solitude of my own apartment.

UNTIL I joined the air force, I'd always thought of myself as a relatively neat and orderly person. I didn't go to ridiculous lengths—like aligning my cupped bras at precise angles to my tightly rolled panty hose or folding my panties into three-inch squares. But I did cram the aforementioned undergarments into various drawers. Most of the time. I even transferred my dirty dishes from the sink to the dishwasher on a more or less regular basis.

Officer Training School showed me the error of my ways. For those hellish months everything I owned, and I mean *everything*, had to be cupped or rolled or squared.

After OTS I suffered a severe allergic reaction to precise and orderly. So I unlocked my front door that hot August afternoon and hauled my gear into a comfortable jumble of old newspapers, scattered magazines, dusty plants and discarded flip-flops.

It's a a small apartment, half the size of the one Charlie and I had rented in Vegas, but close to Fort Bliss. It's also the most I can afford on a second lieutenant's pay. Lest you think I'm overdramatizing, Google up the U.S. military pay scale sometime. You'll be shocked at our paltry remuneration. I certainly was.

That bit of editorializing aside, I'm actually pretty comfy with one bedroom, bath, kitchen and the tiny eating area I've set up as an office of sorts. The kitchen has new appliances and the floors throughout the apartment are tile. Best of all, the sliding glass doors in the living room open right onto the pool and barbeque pit.

As mentioned above, the apartment complex is close to Fort Bliss, which has a large transient population, so most of the residents are young couples or singles. Consequently, both the pool and the pit get a real workout on weekends. Depending on the amount of beer consumed, bathing suits may or may not become optional.

This early in the afternoon, however, a suit was required. Craving a cool dip after the drive in from the site, I changed into my skimpy little two-piece and dived in. I did three lengths of the pool—my nod to physical fitness—then floated on a foam raft until thirst drove me back inside.

As I showered and shampooed off the chlorine, I couldn't help remembering my last shower in the same stall. I had yet to shake my residual guilt over those stolen hours at home while an unseen arsonist stalked my site. Despite the guilt, it felt wonderful to be squeaky clean and boot-free for the rest of the weekend.

I pulled on a pair of gray jersey shorts with a drawstring waist and a T-shirt I'd cut off to leave my midriff open and cool. Barefoot, I padded into the kitchen. If I hadn't had that blasted report hanging over my head, I would have poured a glass of wine and settled in to peruse the magazines that had piled up during my absence.

I subscribe to a number of glossies. They're my one vice. Okay, one of my vices. My favorites are *People*, *Cosmo*, *allure* and *Elle*. What can I say? I'm a girl.

I also love *21*. If you're not familiar with the title, it's a slick amalgamation of luxury lifestyles, travel, fashion and global gaming. My lifestyle is a *long* way from luxurious and I doubt I'll stroll into the glittering casinos in Baden-Baden or Monte Carlo anytime soon. But *21* was more or less compulsory reading for anyone who lived or worked in Vegas. Now I'm hooked.

By the way, I'm sure you noted that none of the above magazines contain a hint of anything remotely resembling science or research. Both Pen and Rocky have offered to supplement my reading material on numerous occasions. So has O'Reilly, for that matter, but my recreational taste differs substantially from his so I've graciously declined all offers.

I gave the pile of magazines a look of intense longing as I popped an individual-size frozen lasagna in the microwave. I'd made a quick stop at Panera's on the way home so I had low-fat black bean soup, a Greek salad and a crusty baguette to round out my meal.

I ate it at the table that doubled as my desk, savoring every bite as long as I could before I dumped the dishes in the sink. There they would sit for the rest of the weekend, my declaration of independence from neat and orderly.

I heard noises outside and had to battle the urge to join the Friday night crowd. Instead, I dragged out my briefcase and set up my laptop. Didn't take long until I was once again up to my ears in property inventories and Chapter Seven reporting requirements. While I was hammering out what I hoped was the final draft of my report, my cell phone pinged.

I recognized O'Reilly's number and experienced an instant frisson of alarm. Shows you how shell-shocked I was by our recent string of disasters. I'd last seen O'Reilly driving off with Noel and was envisioning both of them caught in tangled wreckage or hijacked by banditos when I flipped my phone open.

"What's up, Dennis?"

"Are you near a TV?"

"Huh?"

"A television. Are you near one?"

I glanced at the set sitting mute in the living room.

"Yes."

"Turn on Channel Six. Now!"

CHAPTER EIGHT

I hit the remote and tuned into Channel Six. A perky blond reporter holding a microphone in front of her face morphed into view.

"... in the death of Patrick James Hooker, the American mercenary accused of selling stolen arms to drug lords. Three U.S. Marines and six Colombian paramilitary officers died in an ambush when those arms were turned against them. Special Agent Paul Donati from the FBI's El Paso field office provided the details."

The camera zoomed to a phalanx of uniformed law enforcement types and plainclothes officials standing on the steps of the federal courthouse. Front and center was the trim, wavy-haired FBI agent I'd met in the back room at Pancho's.

A very familiar Border Patrol agent was next to him. Jeff Mitchell stood at a loose parade rest, his arms clasped behind him and his face unreadable as Donati spoke into a bank of microphones.

"Working from a list of personnel who'd either been stationed with or were friends of the three marines who died in Colombia, FBI agents across the country conducted a series of interviews."

So Dan-O or his boss had come through with the names Mitch requested. The Constitution must have weighed as heavily on his shoulders as it had on mine! Shoving aside a pile of yet-to-be-read magazines, I dropped on the sofa and curled my legs under me.

"Those interviews led us to Mr. John Armstrong," Donati continued. "Mr. Armstrong lost his only son, Gunnery Sergeant John Armstrong Jr., in a similar raid two months previously. Mr. Armstrong at first denied any involvement in Hooker's death, but his neighbors indicated he became increasingly angry after the charges against Hooker were dismissed. One neighbor quoted him as vowing 'to make things right.' We then obtained a search warrant and matched a boot in Mr. Armstrong's closet to a print found at the scene."

Well, whaddaya know! EEEK and ole Rock's data synthesizer had provided the evidence that cracked the case. I basked in a reflected glow of pride for my team's sleuthing skills as Donati continued.

"At that point we advised Mr. Armstrong of his rights. He then confessed to shooting both Patrick Hooker and Juan Sandoval."

The guy confessed? That would save the government big bucks on what would no doubt have become a sensational trial. I might even have been called as a witness. I was feeling a little miffed again at missing out on my few minutes of fame when the camera cut back to the reporter.

"FBI agents arrested Armstrong at his ranch outside Sierra Blanca earlier this afternoon. He was brought to the El Paso County Jail for booking and transport to a federal containment facility."

The next scene showed a white-haired, handcuffed individual being led into the jail, flanked by a platoon of uniformed and plainclothes officers. As is typical of so many in this part of the country, the sun had baked his lined, craggy face to leather. His shoulders were hunched and he kept his head down to avoid the cameras. But when another reporter dropped a boom mike a foot from his face and yelled a question, his chin snapped up.

"Yeah, I shot 'em," he shouted back, his eyes as savage as his voice. "Murdering bastards, both of them. They and their kind killed my son. They deserved to die."

Ooooh-kay.

I wanted to sympathize with a man who'd lost his only son to druggers but to tell you the truth, Armstrong looked and sounded more than a little scary . . . until the man's shoulders slumped and tears began to course down his leathery cheeks. Then he just looked like a broken-hearted father.

The perky blond reporter embellished on that image in the clips that followed. Several neighbors and friends talked about Armstrong's devastation at the loss of his son, his loneliness after his wife died of cancer, his increasing bitterness over a flawed justice system that would release a murdering renegade like Hooker. The reporter confirmed Armstrong had written several scathing letters to the editor calling for impeachment of bleeding heart, left-wing judges like the one who'd ordered Hooker's release, and he had talked about petitioning the White House to intervene.

The last clip panned across a small, dust- and wind-swept country cemetery before zooming in on the meticulously tended graves of Margaret Catherine Armstrong and her son, John Armstrong Jr. The last image viewers saw was the small American flag planted beside Gunnery Sergeant Armstrong's grave whipping in the wind.

Effective. *Very* effective. I'd felt sorry for an obviously grieving father a few moments ago. Now I was ready to whip out my checkbook and contribute to his defense fund.

"In other news . . ."

I hit the remote and surfed the channels. I caught bits and pieces of the story on all local channels, with more details promised at ten.

O'Reilly called again while I was surfing. I could hear him clicking a keyboard while he peppered me with questions via his hands-free phone.

"Did you catch the story?"

"Yeah."

"Whaddaya think? Did Dead Guy Number One get his just deserts?"

"Well . . ."

"That was something about the boot print, wasn't it?"

"Uh-huh."

"Think Armstrong is the one who set fire to our lab? Or hired someone to do it?"

Well, duh! The possibility hadn't occurred to me. I'd been too caught up in all the murder stuff.

"He didn't confess to arson," I pointed out, "only to shooting Hooker and Sandoval."

"Yeah, but the two gotta be connected. Armstrong could have nosed out the identity of the military officer who found the bodies. Learned what kind of testing we do out there at the site. Maybe the old man got a hint through his son's Marine Corps connections that we'd collected data from the murder scene."

I chewed on my lower lip and replayed snippets of my meeting with Dan-O in my head. Squirming a little, I recalled whining about having to put my team's test schedule on hold while we processed data collected at the scene. I couldn't believe Danny would deliberately leak that information to any of his other acquaintances. But then I hadn't intended to leak it, either.

Another possible charge to add to my list of sins! Desertion, liability for the loss of thousands of dollars' worth of government equipment, and now unauthorized disclosure of sensitive investigative information. I was envisioning how I'd look in black-and-white prison stripes when I remembered a law enforcement officer had sat right beside me during the tête-à-tête with Dan-O. Mitch hadn't issued any warnings or reprimands for my slip at the Smokehouse. Nor when he'd called yesterday morning, after the fire.

I had a sudden nasty thought. Maybe that's why Mitch hadn't kept me posted on the unfolding developments as promised. He couldn't trust me not to blab 'em. Or maybe it was more a case of out of sight, out of mind. I didn't particularly care for either alternative.

I thought about calling *him* and asking what gives, but

decided to wait another day or two. I was glad I had when he showed up at my apartment the next evening.

I was once again wearing my favorite gray drawstring shorts but had donned a slightly more reputable red tank top. An Eiffel Tower picked out in sequins was splashed across my breasts, compliments of my previous place of employment.

When I peered through the peephole, it took me a few seconds to recognize the distorted apparition on the other side of the door. His cheeks and chin were stubbled, his eyes bleary. Nary a trace of a green uniform showed at his neck or shoulders.

He must have noticed my eyeball blocking the light from the inside. Scraping a hand over his chin, he ID'ed himself. "It's Mitch, Samantha."

"Could've fooled me," I muttered as I slid back the safety chain.

I don't usually hook the chain. It's not exactly industrial strength and probably wouldn't keep out a determined ten-year-old. Besides, as I think I've mentioned, I live in a friendly apartment complex. Especially on Friday and Saturday nights.

Last night was no exception. But I'd ignored the splashes and other sounds of revelry outside my sliding glass doors and kept my nose to the grindstone. I'd spent hours double-checking inventory numbers and polishing my report. Seeing those long columns of numbers and realizing how much valuable test instrumentation we'd lost to an arsonist really pissed me off. It had also made me just a tad nervous to think someone had deliberately set out to destroy our lab. Thus the peephole and chain.

All thoughts of arson and inventory numbers dissipated the moment I opened the door to Agent Mitchell. Even scruffy and bleary-eyed, the man got to me. Pure reflex had me chanting my personal mantra. The one designed to prevent my hormones from sabotaging my brain.

"Charlie, Charlie, Charlie."

I didn't realize I'd muttered my chant aloud until Mitch leaned a tanned forearm against the doorjamb, a quizzical expression in his gold-green eyes.

"Charlie Who?"

"Charlie Spade. My jerk of an ex. I invoke his name whenever . . . Uh . . ."

I floundered around for an explanation that wouldn't make me sound like a total nympho.

"Whenever men who promise to call me and keep me apprised of unfolding events, don't."

"Sorry 'bout that. Everything happened so fast I didn't have time to call. That's why I'm here. To apologize."

"Oh. Okay. Apology accepted."

I started to ask how he'd tracked me down at home but realized just in time what an asinine question that was. Law enforcement types had access to all sorts of databases unavailable to lesser mortals.

That thought led instantly to another. Did I pay my last speeding ticket? Or the one before that? I must have. Mitch didn't look as though he was ready to slap on a pair of cuffs and haul me down to traffic court.

Although . . . I wouldn't have minded the cuffs part. Especially when a smile crinkled the skin at the corners of his eyes. It wasn't one of his full-out grins, but it came close enough to generate some *extremely* salacious thoughts.

"Can I come in?"

"Sure."

As I indicated before, my place is cozy but small. The addition of a broad-shouldered male shrank it to minuscule proportions. He took a moment to look around. I took the same moment to look at him.

I couldn't fail to note the aforementioned shoulders were encased in a faded navy blue T-shirt that also showcased a very nice set of pecs. The muscular thighs hugged by his well-washed jeans weren't bad, either, but I wondered at the stubble on his cheeks and chin. Ditto the red rimming his eyes.

"Long weekend?"

"Yeah." He rubbed the back of his neck. "After the Armstrong arrest went down, I drove back out to Dry Springs."

"Why?"

"I kept thinking I'd missed something. And I wanted to take a look at your lab. Pretty grim."

"I know. I was there."

I ushered him into the living room, scooped some glossies off the sofa and dumped them on the coffee table.

"Would you like a drink? I don't have anything diet, but I could put some coffee on. Or I have bottles of green tea in the fridge."

He sent me an odd look.

"It's Lipton's," I hastened to assure him. "Not the seaweed and sunflower brew Pen—Dr. England—forced on you out at the site."

I realized I'd misinterpreted his look with his next comment.

"Just out of curiosity, why did you assume I wouldn't want a beer? Or a scotch?"

"I saw what you were drinking at Pancho's."

His eyes narrowed at my deliberately nonchalant tone. "And . . . ?"

"And Tess Garcia mentioned you were fighting your way back from a rough patch."

He started to close up and retreat inside a defensive shell. I recognized the signs. I should. I'd seen them often enough. Reluctantly, I shared some of my less-than-stellar family history.

"I know what those rough spots can do to people, Mitch. My grandfather got drunk and drove a semi into a bridge abutment. My mother and middle brother have both been in AA for years. And I worked my way through college as a cocktail waitress in Vegas. I can tell when someone really wants a drink but won't let himself have it."

He dropped his glance, shielding his eyes and his thoughts for several moments. When his lids lifted again, he nodded to my stretchy tank top.

"You worked at the Paris Casino?"

"Right."

"I lost a bundle there my last trip to Vegas."

He didn't want to talk about whatever had sent him to the bottle. Fine. I could live with that.

"So what will it be?" I quipped, smart-mouthed as ever. "Coffee, tea or me?"

His glance zoomed to my sequined Eiffel Tower again and a real, live grin slipped out.

"Why don't we start with the coffee and see where it goes from there?"

Yowza!

Struggling to remember my ex's name, I retreated to the kitchen. While the coffeemaker gurgled, I extracted the Triple Chocolate Meltdown I'd ordered in a moment of sheer gluttony at the Applebee's on Airway Boulevard. Since I'd also ordered an Ultimate Trio of appetizers, I'd ended up bringing the dessert home and sticking it in the freezer.

I zapped the frozen white chocolate, ice cream and brownie just long enough to make it cuttable into halves. When I returned to the living room with coffee mugs and the sinfully rich dessert, Mitch was flipping through the latest edition of *Cosmo*.

"Five Different Sex Positions to Test on Your Man?" he read aloud. "Confessions of a Hopeless Shoe Addict? Great Summer Glows?"

I bristled and was ready to defend my choice of educational materials when he shook his head.

"I can't believe my wife lets my daughter read this."

I unbristled, intrigued by the comment. Interesting that he didn't brand his former spouse with a big, fat **EX** as I always did. Even more interesting, he had a hitherto unmentioned offspring.

"How old is your daughter?"

"Fourteen."

"She probably reads *CosmoGirl*. It's geared more toward teens."

"God, I hope so!"

"What's her name?"

"Jenny. She lives in Seattle with her mother." His attention swerved to the plates I'd carried into the living room. "That looks good. What is it?"

"Applebee's infamous Triple Chocolate Meltdown."

I settled in at one end of the sofa with my coffee and ice cream. Mitch eased back at the other end. When he hooked an ankle over his knee, I caught a glimpse of a black, Velcro'ed holster.

"You always come armed on visits to friends?"

"We make as many enemies as friends here on the border," he said with a shrug, digging into the Meltdown.

I let him scoop down most of his share before demanding details. "Okay, fella, talk to me about John Armstrong."

Mitch's account pretty well dovetailed with the chain of events described by FBI Agent Donati on Channel Six. Information supplied by the USMC Avenger/Stinger school commandant had led to interviews with various marines, including one who'd served with Gunnery Sergeant Armstrong prior to his death. That interview had in turn led to John Armstrong Sr., who'd kept in touch with members of his son's unit and echoed their disgust over Hooker's release.

What Donati *hadn't* mentioned was that Gunnery Sergeant John Armstrong Jr. had trained as a sniper and had been specifically selected for the joint U.S.-Colombian task force because of that skill.

"Armstrong Jr. spent a couple weeks at home with his folks before shipping out," Mitch said quietly. "He brought his weapon with him. And several cartons of M118LRs. It's against regs to fire those rounds for non-mission-related purposes, but he and his dad were both shooters. According to Armstrong Sr., he talked his son into demonstrating his skill by demolishing cacti at a thousand yards. He also talked him out of a carton of M118LRs as a keepsake."

"Which he used to take out the man he believed responsible for the death of three marines," I murmured. "His version of frontier justice, I guess."

Mitch nodded and set aside his bowl. "No question it was premeditated. Armstrong admitted he'd laid in wait for the two men and took great care to erase his tracks after the shooting."

"Except the boot print EEEK uncovered."

"Except that." Mitch scraped a palm across his jaw. "What bothers me is how Armstrong knew where and when Hooker would try to slip back into the U.S."

"How *did* he know?"

"He says he got an anonymous call. The caller gave him the date, approximate time and place Hooker would cross the border. We checked his phone records and traced the call to a disposable cell phone that's no longer in operation. It was purchased at one of those mall kiosks. Cash transaction, and the purchaser gave a false name and address. The clerk who sold it remembers only sketchy details about the buyer. Male. Caucasian. About five-nine or -ten. Brown hair. My guess is the phone is at the bottom of the Rio Grande right now."

"So someone set Hooker up and let Armstrong do his dirty work for him?"

"That's the current thinking, although we can't completely discount the possibility Sandoval, not Hooker, was the main target."

"Are you going to try to track the caller? Wouldn't he be, like, a conspirator to murder?"

"The FBI's working that, but I didn't sense a whole lot of enthusiasm from Donati. Or anyone else, for that matter. The general consensus seems to be that Armstrong did the country a service by taking out both men."

"I have to say I agree. How about you?"

"I don't like the idea of a father who lost his only child being set up like that."

As he turned to reach for his coffee I caught a flicker of something I couldn't quite interpret in his eyes. It was gone when he faced me again.

"Did Armstrong say anything about firebombing my lab?" I wanted to know.

"No. In fact, he categorically denied knowing anything about the fire."

"You believe him?"

"Yeah, I do. He was ready enough to confess to murder when faced with the evidence. He wouldn't have held back on a little thing like arson."

"That leaves two loose ends." I stirred the mush at the bottom of my bowl with my spoon. "The anonymous call to Armstrong and the fire at my site."

"There's no hard proof the two are related," Mitch reminded me.

"Not yet. But we may find a connection when we dig deeper."

"We?"

"We," I repeated firmly. "I've got a score to settle with whoever put me through the hell otherwise known as Chapter Seven."

"Okay, I'll bite. Chapter Seven of . . . ?"

"Volume Twelve, DOD Manual 7000.14." My voice reverberated with undisguised loathing. "*Financial Liability for Government Property Lost, Damaged or Destroyed.* Damned report took me all weekend!"

"At least you got yours done. I still have to write mine."

Weariness tinged his reply. I added it to his red eyes and stubbled cheeks and firmly repressed any lingering, yowza-type thoughts.

The spark was there. I'd felt it when I opened the door to him. And in the way his glance had lingered on my face during our conversation. But the man was dead on his feet.

"You sound almost as wiped as you look," I told him sympathetically. "Maybe we should call it a night so you could get to your report."

He looked at me with a question in his gold-green eyes. I didn't pretend to misunderstand.

"There'll be a next time," I said.

This from the woman who'd always lived for the moment? Who'd tumbled into and out of marriage in six short months? Who'd reacted to her husband's cheating by marching into an air force recruiting office?

I was amazed at this new, restrained me, although the

regret on Mitch's face as I walked him to the door came perilously close to undercutting my decision. That, and the knuckle he curled under my chin.

"Next time," he promised, tipping my face for a kiss that curled my toes.

CHAPTER NINE

I rolled out of bed, pulled on my uniform and departed my apartment at the unheard of hour of six A.M. Monday morning. I wanted to beat the traffic and have time to look over my report one last time before zinging it off to my boss.

I wasn't consciously attempting to demonstrate my thoroughness and dedication to duty. Still, I *did* nourish a secret hope Dr. J would note the time of dispatch and be suitably impressed.

The sun was just beginning to bathe the Franklin Mountains in soft dawn light when I drove through the main gate of Fort Bliss. Did I mention that FST-3's suite of offices is located in the historic section of the post?

The original garrison was established in 1848 to protect settlers from marauding Comanches and Apaches. General Black Jack Pershing launched his raid on Pancho

Villa from here in 1916. He's the guy the Pershing Missile System was named for, in case you didn't know. I didn't, until I toured the post museum on a slow afternoon.

Here's another bit of trivia I picked up at the museum. Fort Bliss is named for Lieutenant Colonel William Wallace Smith Bliss. A West Point grad and veteran of the Mexican-American War, W.W. married Miss Betty, the daughter of Major General and later President Zachary Taylor. What's interesting is that W.W. never set foot on this particular patch of Texas dirt. Guess if you marry the boss's daughter you don't have to be present to have a military installation named after you.

Fort Bliss has always been predominantly army but does have ties to my branch of the service. Briggs Airfield, one of the very first flying fields, was established here in 1919. Back in the day, Briggs handled blimps, B-17s, B-29s, B-36s, B-47s, and B-52s. For those of you not familiar with military prefixes and numerology, "B" stands for bomber. Don't be embarrassed. The prefix didn't register with me, either, until months after I'd donned an air force uniform.

Following WWII, German scientists dubbed "the prisoners of peace" began arriving at Fort Bliss to work on American missile development. Coming from a country where it rains more often than not, I can only guess what they must have thought of our searing blue skies and sunscorched desert topography.

Since those early days, Bliss has grown into the army's premier missile training center . . . and the home of FST-3. We're housed in a thirties-era building that's been renovated at least a dozen times over the decades.

Renovation dollars come out of Operations and Maintenance funds, you see. O&M is a different pot from New Construction, which requires congressional approval. Thus, it's easier to gut a facility and rebuild it from the inside out than construct a new one. The problem is, you're still left with the same exterior shell and limited square footage. All this was explained to me by a rather exasperated deputy post commander when I voiced a number of complaints about our cramped quarters.

After my team's quarterly expeditions to CHU-ville, however, our 1930s building always assumes the aura of a well-loved architectural work of art. This morning was no exception. I gazed fondly at the two-story edifice as I parked the Bronco in the lot across the street.

I then took the unusual precaution of locking it. Not because I feared anyone would steal it. Truth was, I prayed every night this collection of rusted dents would disappear so I could file an insurance claim for whatever it was worth. No, my concern this morning was EEEK, who'd taken up semipermanent residence in the back of my Bronco until I could ship him to Harrison Robotics in Phoenix.

Since I was first in, I flipped on lights, powered up computer systems and made coffee. With luck, I could swill down a half a pot before Pen arrived and badgered me into switching to tea.

My luck held. By the time my team straggled in just before eight A.M., I was on my third cup and had sent my loss/damage report winging through cyberspace to Dr. J at DARPA Headquarters.

O'Reilly stuck his head in my office first. Since we'd returned to post and had to maintain at least a semi-professional image, he'd exchanged his T-shirt and wrinkled cargo shorts for a polo shirt and wrinkled Dockers.

"Greetings, oh Princess of Putterers."

"Hi, Dennis."

"Morning confab as usual?"

We'd formed the habit of gathering at the start of each workday to coordinate schedules and discuss ongoing projects. Since many of those projects involved unbelievably wacky inventions, our morning gathering often produced groans, howls or hoots of laughter that had started some weird stories circulating about FST-3 among the other occupants of the building.

"Confab as usual," I confirmed.

I wasn't sure when we'd go out to Dry Springs for testing again. I might have to work out an alternate site for less sophisticated tests. In either case, we needed to continue to assess items submitted for evaluation and line up those that might by some wild stretch of the imagination have potential for military application.

The team crowded into my cubbyhole of an office a few minutes later. Pen had spiffed up for our return to civilization by exchanging her Birkenstock sandals for Birkenstock clogs and several layers of natural fiber linen. A pair of ebony Chinese chopsticks anchored her lopsided bun. Rocky wore a summer seersucker suit. Sergeant Cassidy, like me, was in ABUs.

Before getting down to business, we rehashed the news from Friday night. My team's reactions to Armstrong's arrest and confession ran the gamut. Pen shook her head over the tragedy of it all. Noel Cassidy thought Armstrong deserved a medal for taking Hooker out. O'Reilly wanted to dissect every gory detail. Rocky fretted about whether the murders were connected to the fire at the lab.

I was careful not to reveal the additional information Mitch had shared last night. I wasn't sure how much of it was sensitive, and contrary to my mother's frequent assertions, I *do* learn from past mistakes. But that business about the mysterious phone call to Armstrong came to mind later, during our confab.

The review session produced more hoots and howls than usual. They were probably a release mechanism or reaction to the stress of losing our lab. But I defy anyone to keep a straight face while listening to Pen read the specs on artificial sweat or Rocky try to explain the intricacies of an emergency evacuator.

One submission got me thinking, however. Always a dangerous occupation on my part, although I had no idea how dangerous in this instance.

The inventor claimed to have come up with a surefire way to retrieve digitized voice patterns from ordinary cell phones, then match them to fingerprints and iris scans for a biometric signature 20–30 percent more accurate than DNA. This project was clearly outside our charter of evaluating inventions with potential for use in desert terrain, but as I said, it got me thinking.

"Didn't we receive another submission along these same lines a few months ago?" I asked my team. "As I recall, the inventor proposed a methodology to retrieve signals from a quiescent device."

"Totally different concepts," Rocky asserted. "The methodology you're talking about involved powering up telematic units using remote command signals."

"Didn't the command signal include a unit identifier?

"Yes."

"And the command information could be uplinked from one of several sources, right?"

"Correct."

"Give me the case number, will you? I want to pull it up and take another look at it."

"Why?"

That's the thing about working with brainiac civilians. They always want explanations. I didn't want to blab about the phone call Armstrong Sr. received, so I fobbed my test engineer off with a half-truth.

"Before I decide whether we should evaluate this new submission, I want to review our rationale for disapproving the other."

"They're completely different concepts," Rocky reiterated. "And we didn't disapprove it. We bounced it to FST-1."

"What did they do with it?"

"They disapproved it."

"Just get me the case number. Puh-leez."

That's another thing about civilians. Nice works better than tough. Sometimes.

Rocky duly sent the case number to my desktop computer and I pulled up the file. The specs soon crossed my eyes. There were pages and pages of 'em, all written in excruciating technicalese. But the bottom line was that the inventor, one Girja Singh, claimed to have fabricated a way to retrieve signals from a telemetric device dropped in the Bering Sea and now thought to be buried somewhere under the polar ice cap. The very expensive device was supposed to have tracked the migration of harp seals, which related to naval operations in a way I couldn't quite grasp.

My team had no desire to go polar so we'd forwarded the submission to our sister team up in the Alaskan tundra. FST-1 had made an attempt to evaluate the invention but gave it up when one of their team members developed a severe case of hypothermia while testing the device. FST-1 did, however, indicate the invention might merit further study . . . sometime in the distant future.

You've probably figured out my rationale. If this handy-dandy invention could, in fact, retrieve signals from a stone-cold dead device buried under tons of ice, maybe it could pick up signals from a cell phone Mitch speculated was now at the bottom of the Rio Grande. I knew it was long shot but what the heck.

I noted Mr. Singh's email address. Or was Girja a Ms.? I wasn't sure so I sent a gender-neutral email asking the inventor to contact me for a possible re-evaluation. I included my name, title, duty address and phone number. After clicking send, I got down to business.

THE next few days passed in a blur of activity. Dr. J acknowledged receipt of my report and said he would appoint an inquiry officer. He also told me the CID had confirmed their suspicion of arson. With great relief, I jettisoned all worry about being held personally or fiscally responsible for the damage to the lab.

I wasn't quite as successful at jettisoning EEEK. I emailed All Bent several times with no response, then tried to reach him by phone. Don't you hate it when people don't respond to emails? Playing telephone tag is *so* twentieth century.

When the messages I left on his voice mail also went unanswered, I contacted the president of Harrison Robotics. He informed me Mr. Benson had suffered an unfortunate accident while demonstrating a robotic-driven wheelchair to a client. I informed *him* that his Ergonomic Exoskeletal Extension had taken up residence in the back of my Bronco due to an unfortunate accident at our test site.

I offered to send EEEK home by FedEx or UPS or camel, but the prez promised to make the necessary arrangements . . . after he consulted with All Bent about the device's condition and usability. I think he'd heard about the goop decorating EEEK's foot pedals and wasn't sure he wanted his expensive piece of equipment back anytime soon.

That left me trying to find someplace to stash EEEK and the equipment we'd salvaged from the lab. I also needed to find an alternate facility, one that would allow FST-3 to conduct at least limited evaluation and testing until we were fully operational again.

I sucked it in and called the deputy post commander. This was the same harried individual I'd complained to previously about our cramped quarters, so I wasn't too surprised when he said he'd look into the matter and get back to me. I figured I'd hear from him by next July. If then.

I then turned the problem over to Sergeant Cassidy, which is what I should have done in the first place. NCOs have a spy network that makes the CIA look like bumbling amateurs. Took him all of a half hour to appropriate a portion of a storage room in the base gym. Not surprising, as he spent most of his off-duty hours there.

The room was locked and only accessible by gym personnel. Still, I suffered severe qualms about depositing EEEK there. I had visions of some muscle-bound jock springing him out of his container and challenging him to a one-on-one on the basketball court or track. I just knew I would look out my window and see him bounding down the road beside some sweating troop.

Despite my doubts, I left him amid the other equipment we'd hauled away from the lab. With the equipment locked up amid volleyball nets and cartons of toilet paper, Noel promised to get to work finding an interim test facility.

HE was still searching on Wednesday morning, when I received a copy of the CID's interim report. As Dr. J had indicated, it confirmed their suspicion of arson but one of the items in the report sent me across base to consult with the unsmiling young De Niro look-alike.

His real name was Jerald Hansen and he operated out of Fort Bliss's main fire station. Jerry talked me through the technical aspects of his report. I listened, pretending I understood, then zeroed in on the part that had caught my attention.

"You say here you think the short circuit that sparked the fire was remotely activated."

"That's right."

"How?"

He flipped to a photo of what looked like a melted plastic bubble. "This is a new generation of infrared light-emitting diode. It works like your TV remote," he added at my blank look. "It can be activated by any signal sent via a variety of devices."

"Like a cell phone?" I asked with a sudden hitch in my breath.

"Sure."

He launched into a complicated explanation of electromagnetic pulses as trigger devices that Rocky would have grasped intuitively. Needless to say, it went right over my head. All I was interested in was that bit about the cell phone.

I'm a great believer in coincidence. Why else would Charlie Numnutz Spade have suggested we hit the Tunnel of Love Drive-Through Wedding Chapel on September 10, when I was feeling a sort of sappy sentimentalism? It sure as heck wasn't because he remembered—or even knew!—the 10th is my birthday.

But this was too much for mere coincidence. A call to a grieving father made from a disposable cell phone, alerting him to where and when Hooker would try to slip back into the country. Another call from a similar device destroys data collected at the scene of Hooker's demise.

The inescapable connection whizzed around in my head as I drove back across base. I had to stop at an intersection and wait while a Patriot missile convoy rumbled past, heading out to the range for a test fire. Since arriving at Fort Bliss I've learned that Patriot is an acronym for Phased Array Tracking Radar to Intercept of Target. Or, if you prefer the troops' version, Protection Against Threats, Real, Imagined, or Theorized.

By either name, the Patriot doesn't look like much from the outside: a long, rectangular box mounted on trucks or trailers they call caissons. As in "When the cai-ssons go roll-ing along, dum-da-dum." Inside those innocuous-looking boxes, though, were six to eight launch tubes containing lethal missiles. Hopefully, no one will ever aim one of those suckers in my general direction.

The last caisson cleared the intersection and I fought heroically to stay within the post's 25 mph speed limit for the rest of the way to my office building. I re-entered the blessed air-conditioned cool, removed my hat and stuffed it into the leg pocket of my ABUs. Brushing back the sweat-dampened tendrils that insist on escaping my hair clip, I approached what we laughingly call the FST-3 waiting area. This consists of two plastic chairs wedged side-by-side in the hall outside my cubbyhole of an office.

Many an inventor has planted his or her butt on those plastic chairs. Some came to provide supplemental information on projects submitted for evaluation. Some came to rant at me for heartlessly rejecting their babies.

I wasn't sure which category the slight, dark-haired female in jeans and a T-shirt fell into. She looked to be no more than fifteen or sixteen years old. She had a visitor's pass clipped to her T-shirt, which meant one of my team had cleared her for access to our area. Nevertheless, I approached cautiously. Even the most unprepossessing inventors have been known to froth at the mouth and exhibit maniacal behavior in defense of their projects.

She looked up at my approach. Her black eyes zeroed in on the name tag on my uniform and a polite, expectant smile lit her face.

Big relief. It didn't look like this visitor was out to maim or dismember or otherwise disfigure me.

"May I help you?"

"I hope so."

Her olive skin and black hair had made me suppose she was a native of West Texas or New Mexico, but her voice had a musical accent I couldn't quite place.

"I am Girja Singh. You emailed me several days ago."

The light dawned. That was British English I was hearing, or more correctly Indian or Pakistani English.

"Yes, I did." I replied. "But I was just looking for information. I didn't expect you to fly in from . . ." I searched my mind for the mailing address on her project submission. "Oregon."

"I live in Oregon, but I attend UCLA," she explained. "We had a week's break between summer and fall sessions, so I decided to drive over and personally demonstrate ALP's capabilities."

As an editorial note, I should point out that the military isn't the only establishment given to acronyms. The academic community is almost as bad. And scientists . . . Lord! You wouldn't *believe* how they love to string together ten or fifteen letters, toss 'em out at random, and automatically assume everyone else understands them.

I tried to remember what ALP stood for but came up blank. Luckily, Ms. Singh fell into the scientist category and assumed I knew.

"I brought ALP with me," she said in her melodious voice. "I shall be most happy to demonstrate it for you."

When she reached into her purse, I expected her to pull out a set of car keys and go outside to retrieve her invention. Instead she withdrew what looked like an ordinary Walkman and a headset with rubberized earpieces, an attached mike, and a telescopic antenna.

"That's it?" I asked. "That's ALP?"

"It is. Did you not review the specs? I included technical drawings and circuitry diagrams."

I wasn't about to admit that her pages and pages of specs had defeated me long before I got to any drawings. I dodged the question with one of my own.

"Mind if I ask how old you are?"

"I am seventeen."

"And you're an undergrad at UCLA?"

"Actually, I am a second year graduate student, working on a master's in electro-acoustical physics."

I did a big gulp and invited Ms. Singh into my office. To shield us both from my ignorance, I also invited Rocky, Pen and Dennis. Sergeant Cassidy, I was informed, had left for an appointment with his shrink.

I introduced Ms. Singh to my team and ignored their puzzled looks as they tried to figure out why I was so interested in a project we'd foisted off on FST-1 months ago. I would tell them about the CID report later. Right now I wanted Ms. Singh to explain in layman's terms how her invention could retrieve signals from a dead telemetric device.

Needless to say, she lost me in the first sixty seconds.

Dennis's eyes glazed over two minutes later. He's into software, not dual mode digital signal processors and geostationary satellite uplink capacity.

Pen and Rocky hung in there, but by the time slender, ultra-serious Girja Singh wound up her supposedly nontechnical explanation, Rocky was fidgeting nervously in his corner and Pen was nibbling the eraser of the pencil she'd plucked from her about-to-fall-down bun.

I couldn't help myself. I had to ask. "Have you thought about working for the government when you finish grad school, Ms. Singh? DARPA could use someone with your smarts."

Her smile was polite but noncommittal.

"About ALP." She opened the disk-shaped Walkman to reveal a palm-size computer with an oval screen and circular keyboard. "Do you wish me to demonstrate its capabilities?"

"Hang on a sec."

I flipped up my cell phone and scrolled to the numbers I'd entered after my first face-to-face with Agent Jeff Mitchell. He answered on the second ring.

"Hi, Samantha."

Isn't Caller ID a wonderful invention? Wish FST-3 could take credit for it.

"Hi there."

I was still in cautious mode, not sure how much of what Mitch had told me I should share with my team. I hadn't seen anything on the news about the anonymous call Mr. Armstrong received. Could be the FBI was still working it.

"What's up?" he asked.

"You know that disposable cell phone you think might be at the bottom of the Rio Grande?"

That was innocuous enough, considering the others in the office didn't know who I was talking to.

"Yeah. What about it?"

"Do you have its number handy?"

"I can get it," Mitch replied. "Why?"

"I'll explain later. Call me back with the number, okay? ASAP."

He remained silent for a moment or two before giving a cautious, "Okay."

I hung up and smiled at Ms. Singh. She smiled back. Rocky twitched. Pen nibbled on her pencil. Dennis looked at me, at the ceiling, at the entrance to my office, as if plotting his escape. We all heaved a sigh of relief when my cell phone buzzed.

"It's Mitch. Ready to copy?"

"Shoot."

He rattled off the number and I promised to get back to him later. I relayed the number to Ms. Singh. She extended what turned out to be a monster telescopic antenna before positioning the earpieces. After clicking a few keys on the circular keyboard, she spoke the number into the headset's mike.

"It's ringing," she announced calmly a few seconds later.

CHAPTER TEN

MY mouth hanging open, I took the headset Ms. Singh handed me. I almost knocked Dennis's glasses off trying to maneuver the antenna and earned an evil glare as he straightened the black frames.

I expected to hear a normal ringtone. What I got was a static-filled brrrrh. I listened for ten seconds or so, half hoping, scared to death that someone might actually answer. I framed a dozen different responses in that short eternity, the most intelligent of which was "Uh, who's this?"

To my disappointment and secret relief, the brrrrh continued unabated.

"There's no answer," I said to the room at large.

"Is the telemetric device you're trying to reach operable?" Ms. Singh asked.

"We don't think so."

"Then why would you expect an answer?" Her dark eyes looked at me reproachfully. "ALP cannot raise the dead. All it can do it tap into the instrument's residual signal capacity, if any still exists."

"Is that what I'm hearing? Residual signal capacity?"

"It is."

"And ALP can pinpoint the location of these signals?"

She was too polite to roll her eyes but I could tell she wanted to. Reclaiming her baby, she tapped a key. My entire team crowded around to look over her shoulder as a series of numbers and letters appeared in the oval display. Even I, the only certified non-techie present, could recognize GPS coordinates when they smacked me in the face.

"Quick! I need to write down these coordinates."

Rocky snatched a notepad off my desk and Pen offered her nibbled-on pencil. The pencil was a little slippery but I wrapped my fingers around it without hesitation. I share a CHU with Dr. Penelope England during our quarterly excursions to Dry Springs, remember? Having been subject to her excessive passion for things natural and organic, I can state with utter confidence that her saliva is safer than the drinking water in all fifty states.

"Dennis, fire up my computer. Let's enter these coordinates and see where they are."

Ms. Singh let out a long sigh. "ALP has built-in satellite mapping capability." She tapped another key and a red star popped up on the screen.

"Zoom out," I requested.

Two lines appeared.

"Again."

The lines resolved into Highway 54 as it snaked across the border of Texas and New Mexico.

There was no river anywhere in sight. The possibility that the phone used to contact Mr. Armstrong might not be at the bottom of the Rio Grande or any other body of water sent a frisson of excitement down my spine.

"Zoom out one more time."

Towns appeared. El Paso to the south. Orogrande, New Mexico, to the north. Dry Springs at the far edge of the map to the east.

We all leaned in for a closer look. Rocky's bony elbow dug into my side. Pen came close to putting out my eye with a Chinese chopstick. Dennis stated what was now obvious to us all.

"Looks like the device emitting these residual signals is in the middle of the desert. This spot's almost as isolated as CHU-ville." His glance cut to me. "What's this all about, Lieutenant?"

"I'll tell you later. Ms. Singh, would you consider leaving ALP with us for further evaluation? Dr. Balboa will be happy to assist you with the necessary paperwork."

Rocky blinked but took the hint and escorted the young woman out of my cubbyhole and down the hall to his. That left Pen and Dennis staring at me with intense curiosity.

"Hang on," I told them. "I need to relay this information. Then we'll get Rocky back in here and I'll explain all."

I dialed Mitch's number again. He answered on the first ring.

"What's going on, Samantha?"

"That disposable cell phone you're looking for? I know where it is."

"Are you serious?"

"Is a pig pork?"

That was pretty lame but I was too excited for my usual witty repartee. Mitch only grunted.

"The FBI says the device is dead. How the hell did you locate it?"

"Too complicated to go into over the phone."

Which was my way of saying I wasn't up to explaining ALP to another non-techie.

"Got a pencil? I'll give you the exact location."

I rattled off the coordinates and posed the sixty-four-thousand-dollar question.

"Can I tell my team why you're looking for the phone?"

"Okay, but advise them to keep it close-hold unless and until I say otherwise."

"Will do. And . . ."

Too late. He'd already cut the connection. I swallowed my request that he keep *me* advised about ongoing events. Personally. Say, over dinner. Any night this week or next.

I had to rein in Pen and O'Reilly's impatience until Rocky finished with Ms. Singh and escorted her out of the building. Luckily, Sergeant Cassidy returned from his appointment just as I was about to Tell All, thus sparing me the necessity of repeating myself later.

My team grasped the significance of the anonymous phone to Mr. Armstrong right away. Noel spoke for them all when he swore and shook his head in disgust.

"Someone set the old guy up."

"That's what Mitch—Agent Mitchell—thinks."

"What kind of heartless bastard would play on a father's grief and incite him to commit murder?"

"Maybe the same heartless bastard who used a cell phone to remotely detonate the fire in our lab."

I showed them the arson investigation report and told them about my earlier visit to the fire department. We spent the rest of the morning in animated, if fruitless, speculation as to who had made the calls.

My office phone rang in mid-afternoon. I picked up, wondering if Mitch had decided to use a land line to let me know the results of his treasure hunt. I had to stifle a severe pang of disappointment when the caller identified himself as Lieutenant Colonel Bob Williams.

I knew him by name if not by sight. He's one of those program managers I told you about. The kind who sit in a big office at DARPA Headquarters and managed trillion-dollar projects at major universities and research centers. As opposed to moi, stuck out here in . . .

Never mind. No point in more whining. You've heard enough of it.

"Hi, Colonel Williams. What's up?"

"Your test lab, according to Dr. Jessup. He's tagged me to conduct the official inquiry."

"Oh. Right. Did he happen to give you a copy of the interim CID report?"

"He did."

I didn't bother to suggest an official inquiry might be superfluous given evidence of arson. During my thirteen months in uniform, I'd learned the hard way that reason and logic always yield to rules and regulations.

"I'll be arriving in El Paso Friday morning at nine-twenty," Colonel Williams informed me. "Delta flight 817."

"Delta flight 817. Got it."

"I'd like you to pick me up and drive out to the site with me."

"Yes, sir."

"See you Friday."

I spent the rest of the afternoon on DARPA's website, reading about the projects Colonel Williams had in the works.

No, I didn't intend to kiss ass! But neither did I want to sound like a total airhead during the long drive out to Dry Springs.

I have to say the colonel was working some impressive programs. Like a Constant Volume Combustion engine capable of delivering twelve thousand pounds of payload up to nine thousand nautical miles in less than two hours. And, at the opposite end of the spectrum, the world's smallest UAV. That's Unmanned Aerial Vehicle to you non-military types. Or to use the vernacular, a remote-controlled drone.

This particular UAV was less than three inches long, flapped its wings like a blood-sucking mosquito and—brace yourself!—was the result of a $1.7 million Phase One brain-storming project. I gaped at the insect-like vehicle and wondered what would prevent some hungry sparrow from deciding it was supper.

I was still perusing Colonel Williams's projects when Mitch called. My pulse kicked into overdrive as I recognized his number on my cell phone's digital display. I flipped up the lid and wasted no time on preliminaries.

"Did you find it?"

"We did." His voice reverberated with satisfaction. "Looks like someone removed the memory card and put a boot heel to the case, but the circuit board was more or less intact. Must have been how you picked up those residual signals."

"Must have."

"Paul Donati wants to talk to you about that."

"No problem. Tell him I'm available for consultation any day but Friday."

"Why not Friday?"

"I have to go back out to the site."

"For how long?"

"I'm not sure. Probably just the day. Why?"

"No reason."

I mulled that over for a moment before asking, "Will the pieces of the phone provide any additional evidence as to who made the call to Armstrong?"

"Too soon to tell, but you can bet the FBI forensics team is going to swipe, spray or sniff every atom of it. I'll let you know if they find anything."

I hung up wondering if I'd imagined that kiss at my place. Agent Mitchell certainly didn't seem in much of a hurry for a repeat performance.

TO my surprise, Dr. J didn't share Mitch's excitement over the found phone . . . or FST-3's role in locating it. He initiated a video-call the following afternoon and looked distinctly uncomfortable at being thrust into what I soon realized was a turf war.

"I received a visit from a Special Agent assigned to CID Headquarters a little while ago, Samantha. He was accompanied by an FBI agent."

"Uh-oh."

"Uh-oh is right. They strongly suggested that any information or evidence relating to an investigation being conducted on U.S. military installations be channeled through them, not the Border Patrol."

"How dumb am I?" I shook my head at my own naivete. "For some reason, I thought all those guys with badges were on the same side."

Dr. J cleared his throat and looked as stern as anyone in a tweedy sport coat and red-checked bow tie could.

"The agents also advised that this case is extremely sensitive, with *very* high level interest."

"Sensitive is right. My nerve endings jump and twitter every time I think about stumbling over those bodies. Good thing I found them, though, or there wouldn't *be* an investigation."

"Yes, well, try to remember to go through proper channels in the future."

"Yes, sir."

I disconnected, my jaw tight. I knew who I owed for that little dressing down. CID agent Hurst aka Comb-Over and I would have a come-to-Jesus meeting. Soon.

I had pretty much gotten over my snit when I left to pick up Lieutenant Colonel Williams at the airport the next morning. Resilience is one of my more positive traits, if I do say so myself. I tend to bounce back quickly from scoldings and reprimands. Probably because I've been on the receiving end of so many.

I wasn't sure how long I'd be out at the site so I packed a cooler with bottled water and stashed some PowerBars in my purse. Advising my team I'd see them when I saw them, I drove to the airport.

The colonel strode out of the gate area looking sharp and senior officer-ish in his service uniform. That's the dark blue one we wear when we're playing dress-up. The silver oak leaves designating his rank gleamed in the bright lights, as did his nickel-coated command pilot wings perched above rows of colorful ribbons.

I suspected those wings wouldn't look anywhere near as bright and shiny after a day of poking around our test site but kept the thought to myself as I shook his hand.

"Good flight, sir?"

"Good enough."

I escorted him to the parking lot. When he caught sight of the Bronc, I got the usual forehead scrunching and disbelieving looks.

"Did the fire damage your vehicle? I didn't see it listed under ancillary items on your report."

"No, sir. It's just, uh, well-seasoned."

With a small grunt, he opened the door and slid into the front seat.

Despite that inauspicious beginning, I enjoyed the drive out to the site. All my prep work paid off. I got the colonel talking about his projects and could actually contribute an intelligent comment once in a while. As I mentioned earlier, he was working some really slick stuff. Even the mosquito drone made sense after he explained its aerodynamics and potential capabilities.

I could tell Dry Springs didn't make much of an impression on him when we drove through. I thought about stopping at Pancho's but decided to save that for the way back. By then the colonel would need feeding and something tall and cool to drink. So would I, although I knew I would have to pull a Mitch and stick to non-alcoholic beverages while chauffeuring a senior officer around.

Colonel Williams appeared even less impressed when we topped the rise that sloped down to CHU-ville. There they sat amid the cholla and scruffy mesquite: the five metal-sided boxes and dinky little storage shed that comprise FST-3's test facility. The colonel didn't say anything but I suspected he was giving silent if fervent thanks for his cushy office in Virginia.

When I pulled up at the site, he shed his coat and tie and rolled up his sleeves. We then spent three hot and distinctly uncomfortable hours while he inspected the fire-ravaged lab and verified the list of equipment we'd declared too damaged to salvage.

"Once I file my inquiry report, you'll need to talk to DRMS about hauling off the CHU," he said when he'd finished poking through the sooty remains. "They might be able to sell what's left of it for scrap."

"Er, DRMS?"

"The Defense Reutilization and Marketing Service. Not sure where the one for this region is located. You can look it up on the Internet."

"Right."

We were both sweating profusely when I padlocked the lab again and we climbed back into the Bronco. Thankfully, the colonel was very much in favor of a stop at Pancho's when we cruised into Dry Springs.

He left his tie and blue jacket with all its shiny accoutrements in the Bronco and followed me inside. I could tell the moment his eyes adjusted to the gloom. He came to a dead stop, swiveled his head, and took in the *Sports Illustrated* decor. He was still admiring the view when Pancho strolled in from the convenience store side of his establishment.

"*Hola*, Lieutenant."

"*Hola*, Pancho."

I delivered the ritual kiss on his cheek and derived some comfort from the familiar, waxy scent of his mustache. I'd never deflate his macho-ness by telling him so, but Pancho has become sort of a father figure to me. Probably because I don't remember much about my own. He disappeared from my life when I was three or four. My mom swears he split on us but I'm pretty sure it was the other way around.

"Who's this?"

I introduced him to the colonel and we took stools at the bar. I ordered iced tea and my usual bowl of green chili stew. Colonel Williams ordered the same.

"So what're you doing in Dry Springs?" Pancho asked as he served the drinks.

"Working the final report of the damage to the lab and our equipment."

I put a slight but intentional emphasis on the word "final." I was certain not even the United States government would require yet another submission. I nourished that foolish hope through two bowls of stew and for a good part of the drive back to El Paso.

En route, the colonel requested I drop him off at the hotel near the airport where he'd reserved a room. He planned to fly back to D.C. tomorrow afternoon, after inspecting the equipment we'd hauled away from the site.

I did a mental squirm but didn't remind him this was Friday evening. Except when we were rusticating in Dry Springs, my team kept more or less regular hours. Weekends they indulged their individual interests.

Rocky had mentioned something about driving up to Albuquerque to visit a fellow engineer who worked at the air force's Space Technology Lab. I wasn't sure what O'Reilly had planned, but I knew that come nine o'clock tomorrow morning Pen would be sitting front row center at the monthly gathering of the El Paso chapter of Scientists for a Safer Environment. She'd dragged me to one meeting. So far I've managed to resist a repeat appearance. I just can't get all worked up over lobbying Congress to classify quantum dots and nanoparticles as a new class of non-biodegradable pollutants.

Taking the coward's way out, I flipped up my phone and hit speed dial for Sergeant Cassidy.

"Hey, Noel. I'm with Colonel Williams. Right. The colonel from Headquarters conducting the inquiry into our damaged equipment. He needs to inspect the items we salvaged tomorrow morning. Yes, tomorrow. Contact the rest of the team. Have everyone assemble at the office at . . ."

I glanced at my passenger for his druthers.

"Oh-six-thirty. That'll give me a good three or four hours to look over the equipment before I have to catch my plane back to D.C."

Gulping, I relayed the time to Noel and left it to him to break the news to my team of dedicated professionals.

CHAPTER ELEVEN

I picked Colonel Williams up at his hotel the next morning and drove him on-post. To my relief, all members of FST-3 showed for early morning roll call. Ignoring their mutters and nasty looks, I introduced them to the colonel.

He must have boned up on resumés before he flew out to El Paso as he had good things to say about Pen's latest paper on fluorocarbons and the software mod Dennis had made to one of DARPA's standardized programs. Sergeant Cassidy got a friendly nod and a returned salute, Rocky a glance that combined wariness and fascination.

"Dr. Balboa. I work with one of your, uh, former colleagues. Dr. Alvin Reed."

The name obviously struck a nerve. Rocky blinked and twitched but stuck out his hand manfully. "Have his eyebrows grown back?"

"Not completely."

I tucked that interesting exchange away for later discussion and herded my troops to the gym. Even at that ridiculous hour, weights clanked and sneakers squeaked on the basketball court. My nostrils twitched at the acrid odor of sweat overlaid with chlorine from the lap pool while we waited for Noel to hunt down someone with a key to the storage room where we'd crammed our salvaged equipment.

We un-crammed it piece by piece so the colonel could compare serial numbers and the equipment's condition to the information I'd sent in. He made several notes in the margins of the report, which started me thinking things like liability and negligent behavior again, but he finished with a reassuring comment.

"Looks like you covered everything adequately in your report, Lieutenant. I'll need an update on what works and doesn't work when you set up and begin testing again."

"Right. We're looking for an interim facility. So far . . ." I glanced at Noel, who shook his head. ". . . no luck."

"Maybe I can help with that. I'll make some calls when I get back to D.C."

He jotted another note in the margin and took a last glance at our scattered equipment. It looked pretty pathetic strung out like that but still represented several hundred thousand dollars in assets.

"That does it for me. Any questions on where we go from here?"

"Just one. Where *do* we go from here?"

I was pretty sure I knew, but I wanted to hear from him when, if ever, I'd be off the hook.

"I'll file my inquiry report for review by the legal office. Then the item managers of the more expensive pieces of equipment will determine which items they want to send to the depot and try to salvage. When they're done with their review, the property manager at Headquarters level will delete the unsalvageable items from your inventory and help you dispose of them. That's where the Defense Reutilization and Marketing Service comes in," he added to jog my memory.

Properly jogged, I nodded. "Sounds like we're talking several weeks yet."

"More like several months."

Of course. Foolish me.

I left the team to re-cram our stuff back into our half of the storage room and drove the colonel to the airport in plenty of time to catch his flight. He'd covered a lot of ground in his day-and-a-half. I hoped the folks who reviewed the results of his inquiry would be as expeditious.

I felt liberated with the colonel gone. The rest of the weekend loomed ahead with nothing more urgent to do than peruse my mags and float in the pool. Or . . .

An alternate plan took shape. On a whim, I flipped up my phone and dialed Mitch.

"Hey, you."

"Hey, back." The smile in his voice generated a little tingle at the base of my spine. "I was just going to call you. What are you doing?"

The tingle moved upward and outward.

"I dropped the inquiry officer off at the airport a few minutes ago and am on my way home. You?"

"Getting ready for two o'clock muster."

Sighing, I jettisoned my half-formed idea of inviting him over for a cool dip followed by hot sex.

"There've been some developments in the Armstrong case," he told me. "I don't want to talk about them over the phone. Where are you now?"

"On Alameda, just passing Fourteenth."

"You're only a couple of miles from my place. Want to swing by?"

"Sure."

He gave me directions, which I followed to a residential neighborhood in the older section of El Paso. The homes were mostly one-story adobe, with lots of swing sets and plastic castles dotting the fenced-in yards. The trees and shrubs were low-water—live oak and Big Bend silver leaf. Buttercup yellow honeysuckle and flaming orange trumpet vine provided splashes of brilliant color.

I had trouble placing tough, no-nonsense Jeff Mitchell in this tranquil setting until I remembered his teenaged daughter. He'd said the girl—Jenny, I remembered—lived with her mother in Seattle. Obviously Mitch kept a home here for when his daughter visited.

Or not.

I realized the error of my thinking after he answered the door and ushered me inside. Blinking, I glanced around the front rooms. The only items in the living room were a beat-up leather sofa and chair, a floor lamp, and a TV. In the dining room, a wrought-iron chandelier dangled above the empty space which should have been filled with a table and chairs. Functional mini-blinds covered the windows in each room.

That was it. No pictures. No swags to soften the stark blinds. No personal touches of any kind except a stack of paperback novels beside the chair.

I glanced up at him. He was in his mean greens and ready for work but I wasn't letting him get away this time without satisfying at least some of my curiosity.

"Lived here long?" I asked dryly.

"About six years."

"Hmmmm."

"I told my wife to haul off everything she wanted when she moved out. She took me at my word."

"When was that?"

"Three years ago."

I lifted a brow, and he shrugged.

"I don't spend much time here. That was one of the reasons my wife moved out," he added, with a wry twist of his lips.

I wanted to ask about the other reasons but Mitch forestalled my nosy questions by playing the polite host.

"How about some coffee? Or ice water? I can manage either."

"Ice water sounds good."

I followed him to the kitchen. It looked a little more lived in, with a coffeemaker, microwave and toaster on the counter and a round oak table positioned to catch the light from the windows.

His bulletproof vest and holstered weapon were hooked over one of the chairs. A mug sat on the table beside a yellow legal pad. The top sheet of the pad contained what looked like a timeline, with dark, heavy arrows leading from one main event to the next. The titles of those events snagged my instant interest.

"Hooker to Armstrong to Bennett to Blank," I read. "Who's Bennett?"

"The owner of the phone we retrieved from the desert."

"The owner? I thought the phone was one of those disposable jobbies, purchased at a mall kiosk and tossed away after one use."

"The number *did* trace to a disposable. Apparently the caller extracted the SIM card containing the phone's registry and traded cases."

"Why?"

"One more attempt to confuse and diffuse, I'd guess."

Mitch clunked ice cubes into a glass, filled it with tap water and joined me at the table.

"The instrument was in pieces and wiped clean except for a partial print under the SIM card. Whoever changed out the card missed that one."

I wasn't surprised. You ever buy a new phone and try to install the SIM card from your old one?

On most phones, you have to unscrew the back cover, remove the battery, locate this little tab thingy the size of a cornflake and ease it out. Non-techie that I am, the task always left me sweating. Or cursing. Or both. It doesn't help matters that my six-year-old nephew can switch one out in eight-point-two seconds. Blindfolded.

"Donati and company ran the print through the FBI's database," Mitch continued. "They came up with more than a hundred and fifty thousand hits."

"A hundred and fifty *thousand*?"

"Like I said, it was only a partial."

"So how did they narrow it to this Bennett character?"

"Donati fed every known variable about Hooker and Armstrong into the Bureau's Statistical Probabilities Analysis System. He looked for links to U.S. Marine Corps snipers, the drug raid in Colombia, the arms deals Hooker supposedly brokered, Juan Sandoval's tattooed ass, and so on. The runs narrowed the possibilities to less than fifty people. Agents then went knocking on doors. One of those doors was Bennett's."

"What's his connection to the case?"

"Her connection."

"I stand corrected. What's *her* connection?"

"She just happens to be a senior analyst at the headquarters of B&R Systems, one of the largest weapons manufacturing conglomerates in the country."

I let out a long, low whistle. "Is that a coincidence, or what?"

"There's more. B&R has had two shipments of arms hijacked in the past six months." Mitch's voice took on a hard edge. "That wouldn't be notable in and of itself. We're seeing almost as many stolen weapons going south these days as drug shipments coming north. What makes these B&R incidents especially significant, though, is that Patrick Hooker was supposedly finalizing the deal for one of those shipments when he was captured."

"No kidding! What did Ms. Bennett have to say about that?"

"According to Donati, she was shocked out of her gourd. Claims she had nothing to do with the stolen shipments, never had any contact with Hooker or anyone associated with him. She also claimed her cell phone was stolen and she didn't have a clue who took it."

He paused for effect.

"Ms. Bennett admitted she'd been having an extramarital affair with a lover who abruptly disappeared from her life two weeks ago. Her phone disappeared about the same time. Donati says they ran every scrap of info Joy Bennett supplied about her lover. Turns out he gave her a fake name, fake address, fake background."

"Wow." I sat back in my chair, amazed at the twists and turns this case had taken. "And all this happened in just a few days. I thought you said Donati and company weren't all that enthused about pursuing the anonymous call to Armstrong Sr. after his confession and arrest."

"Donati got energized when I told him you'd located the phone. He's kept me apprised of what's happened since then. Although . . ." Frowning, Mitch drummed his fingers against his coffee mug. "He called this morning. Said he's getting pressure from the top to screw down the lid on this investigation. Asked me to back off and let him take it from here."

"Interesting. My boss gave me the same line. This was after he received a visit from an agent assigned to CID headquarters. The agent was accompanied by an FBI type. They indicated the case had high level interest. They also indicated they weren't real happy with me for providing those coordinates to a Border Patrol agent instead of channeling them through our military investigative unit."

"That so?" His frown deepened. "I don't understand this posturing. Paul Donati and I go back a long way. We've worked some tough cases together. This is the first time he's ever given in to turf issues pressure."

His gaze dropped to the yellow legal pad and locked on that blank space after Bennett's name. I waited a beat before asking the question I pretty much already knew the answer to.

"You're not going to back off, are you?"

He lifted his gaze. "I can't."

"Why?"

His jaw worked above the collar of his uniform and he hesitated so long I didn't think he would answer.

"They arrested John Armstrong Sr. for murder," he said at last, "but it could have been me. It almost was."

Who has a quip or a quick comeback for a revelation like that? I sure didn't. Uncharacteristically silent, I waited for him to continue.

"I told you I spent a hitch in the navy, right?"

"Yes."

"The long months I spent at sea were tough on my wife. Our marriage started coming apart at the seams, so I left the navy and took a job with the Border Patrol in the hope it would bridge the gulf. The tension between us only got worse but Margo and I hung in there for Jenny's sake."

"Jenny, the Cosmogirl."

"Jenny, the Cosmogirl," he echoed quietly. "She's bright and sweet and the one genuine accomplishment in my life. Or was."

I remembered John Armstrong's anguish at losing his son and got cold all over.

"Wh-What happened?"

"I was on patrol and intercepted some human cargo being smuggled across the border. They were just kids. Eight, ten years old. Scared to death and crying for their mothers." His jaw worked. "Turns out they were destined for a brothel in Houston."

"Oh, no!"

"The more we dug into the situation, the more we realized this was a well-organized and obscenely profitable ring. I asked to work 24/7 with a counterpart in Mexico. Ramon and I went way back. We'd served on a cross-border task force for six months. Took a couple of deep-sea fishing trips together. He had kids, too, and made it a personal quest to shut down this child smuggling operation. Took us months, but we finally ID'ed the ringleader."

His mouth twisted into a hard line.

"Rafael Mendoza. The man's a thug straight from the barrio. He's made so much from peddling human misery that he now has homes in Guadalajara and Mexico City and a seaside condo in Malibu. That's where we nailed him. Sipping champagne and admiring the sunset with his *chica*. When we led him off in handcuffs, Mendoza swore we'd regret taking him down. Ramon's youngest son disappeared a month later."

I got a cramp around my heart and almost didn't want to hear what came next.

I *know* the world's a dangerous place. I *know* it's inhabited by sickos like the one Mitch just described. I'd gotten a taste of sick myself when EEEK and I plowed through Messrs. Hooker and Sandoval. Yet the unquenchable optimism that lands me in trouble more often than not wanted desperately to believe the slime hadn't touched Mitch's daughter.

"Margo, my wife, fell apart when she heard about Ramon's son. She railed at me for putting Jenny's life in danger, for always thinking of my work before my family. She couldn't get out of El Paso fast enough or move far enough away. For Jenny's sake, I had to let them go."

He paused, took a swallow of his now cold coffee and continued.

"I've only seen them twice since. Margo's afraid I'll lead Mendoza's henchmen to Jenny. I'm afraid she's right."

"What? Is he still pulling strings?"

"Yeah, he is. Ramon and I both testified at his trial in Mexico City. Damned thing was a farce from start to finish. He'd obviously bought off the judge and scared the jurors shitless. He should have been sentenced to ten to twenty minimum, but got off with a stiff fine and walked."

"Like Patrick Hooker," I murmured, understanding now.

"Like Patrick Hooker," Mitch echoed grimly. "And, like John Armstrong Sr., I wanted to pump a bullet into the bastard's face so bad I hurt with it."

"But you didn't."

"I may yet, if I sense him or his people getting anywhere close to my daughter."

Or close to him. Mitch hadn't been kidding about making as many enemies as friends in his line of business. No wonder he always walked around with a holster strapped to his ankle.

I understood now why he couldn't let this thing with Armstrong Sr. go. It went too deep, had become too personal.

AS much as I sympathized with Mitch, I left his house with no intention of messing around in the Hooker/Armstrong investigation any further. Honestly!

I'd contributed to Armstrong Sr.'s defense by locating

the cell phone person or persons unknown had called him from. That gave weight to the argument that he'd been set up and might hold some sway with a jury deciding his fate. According to my boss, I needed to let the folks with bright, shiny badges take it from here.

It was mild curiosity that plunked me down in front of my laptop that evening. Idle interest that had me Googling up B&R Systems. Took me all of ten or fifteen minutes to get caught up again in a scary world.

I'm not naive. More to the point, I wear a military uniform. But I had no idea conventional arms was such a humongous, trillion-dollar industry. Or that the U.S. led the pack in sales to other countries, with Russia and the U.K. coming in a distant second and third. We're talking everything from bullets to F-16s here.

Most foreign sales were legitimate and designated for military purposes. But billions of dollars' worth of those armaments ended up on the black market and were sold to the highest bidder. Not F-16s, of course. Those would be kind of hard to auction off on the side. Enough assault rifles, grenade launchers and explosives changed hands, though, to validate Mitch's grim assertion that smuggling arms was becoming as big a business as smuggling dope.

My Googling also confirmed that B&R Systems wasn't the only major weapons producer who'd had their products hijacked. One company lost a whole shipment of armor-piercing bullets. In another grisly report, modern-day pirates had boarded a cargo ship on the open sea and murdered the entire crew to get access to a container of shoulder-launched anti-aircraft missiles.

Chewing on my lower lip, I delved a little deeper into

B&R's history and arsenal of products. The company had started small. A family-owned enterprise, Bauer and Rusk originally manufactured rifles, shotguns, handguns and ammunition for the sporting crowd. Within ten years, B&R had gone public, acquired a rival company, diversified into military armaments and got heavily involved in electronics. Ten years more, and the now international conglomerate was partnering with major defense contractors like Raytheon Missile Systems to produce big-bucks, laser-guided systems capable of taking out all enemies, large and small. Or so the company's literature proclaimed. Last year B&R reported $700 million in profits. Not a bad chunk of change for a company headquartered in some small Arizona town I'd never heard of.

Curiosity got the best of me again. I had to MapQuest Sahuarita, just to see where the heck it was. Right outside Tucson, I discovered.

Just a few hours from Phoenix.

Home of Harrison Robotics.

I stared at the map for long moments. To this day I'm not sure what prompted me to flip up my phone and leave a message on Mitch's cell.

"I don't know what your schedule is next week but I'm thinking of driving over to Phoenix to deliver EEEK to his rightful owners. If you want to go with me, we could make a stop in Tucson, home to B&R Systems, and talk to this Bennett chick."

CHAPTER TWELVE

I pulled into Mitch's driveway at oh-dawn-thirty the following Tuesday morning, only twenty minutes late. These early mornings were turning into a nasty routine.

I had EEEK nested in his shipping container in the rear of my Bronco and a few niggling doubts about my proposed jaunt hovering at the back of my mind.

Dr. J hadn't actually *ordered* me to butt out of the Hooker/ Armstrong investigation. He'd merely suggested it. Strongly. I'm sure there's something in the Uniform Code of Military Justice that would slice right through that thin defense but . . . Well . . .

I kept seeing Armstrong Sr.'s grief-ravaged face when he spoke of his son. And remembering the grim details Mitch had shared about the threat to *his* daughter from some sleazoid trafficker in human misery. Like Mitch, I'd more or less linked the two incidents in my mind.

Then there was the small matter of the destruction of my lab. I took that personally, especially after sweating through that friggin' loss/damage report. Some folks might think it was my obligation, my *duty*, to follow up on any possible connection between the fire and the Hooker/Armstrong case.

And if the trip took longer than expected, if Mitch and I had to spend the night somewhere along the road . . . What can I say? These things happen.

I was envisioning all sorts of potentially delicious scenarios when the lights inside Mitch's place blinked off and he exited the front door.

We'd agreed on civilian clothes for the expedition. I was in hot pink crops and a gauzy tunic swirling with orange and pink poppies. I'd picked up the outfit after splurging half of one paycheck on a Coach tote trimmed in the same sizzling pink. Probably not the best choice for someone with my reddish hair, but out of uniform I crave color. Lots of color. Even my strappy, flat-soled sandals tinkled with bright beads.

Mitch had opted for a more conservative look. Jeans. A white cotton shirt with the cuffs rolled up. A San Antonio Spurs ball cap. When he slid into the passenger seat, the travel mugs he had gripped in one hand smelled as good as he looked.

"Bless you." I reached for one of the mugs with heartfelt gratitude. "I didn't have time to caffeine-up before I left my apartment."

"I figured as much from your flustered call to let me know you were on your way."

He strapped in and I backed out of the driveway with

only a mild tire-squeal. We cleared El Paso's city limits before the rush hour and hit the Texas/New Mexico border just as the sun painted the sky a rosy gold. From there it was a straight shot along I-10 to Tucson. Nothing but three hundred plus miles of desert and small towns like Lordsburg, New Mexico, and Bowie, Arizona, to cruise past.

With all those wide open spaces ahead, my foot got a tad heavy and we ate up the tarmac. My Bronco might look like a demolition derby reject on the outside but it had heart and a new ring job.

To be honest, Mitch contributed far more to making those miles fly by than the Bronco. I sensed we'd crossed a line the other night when he'd explained his identification with John Armstrong Sr. He didn't bring it up again. Neither did I. But it was there with us while we talked through again what we knew of the investigation and, gradually, segued into other, unrelated topics. Like our preferences in literature. And red versus green chili sauce. And country crooners.

The latter led to all kinds of interesting side discussions when a Toby Keith tune popped up on the FM station we'd tuned into.

"How can you not like Toby Keith?" I demanded when Mitch leaned forward to change the station. "You're a Texcan."

"Actually, I didn't move to Texas until I took this job with the Border Patrol. And Toby Keith is from Oklahoma," he pointed out mildly.

I brushed that minor point aside with a flap of one hand. "His music taps into everything important in life. Home. Family. Friday night football."

"A high school football fan, are you?"

"I'll have you know you're looking at a three-year member of the Holderville High dance squad. I was out there every weekend my freshman, sophomore and junior years, twirling those poms."

"What happened senior year?"

"I got a job at the local bistro and decided I really liked having a few shekels in my pocket. Although I have to say all that pom-twirling and tail-shaking came in handy after I moved to Vegas."

"I imagine it would."

I smiled at his solemn reply.

"There's an art to delivering drinks in a place like the Paris Casino," I informed him loftily. "You need to be friendly, but you also have to be careful not to come across as too available."

"I think I speak for most men when I say available is good."

"Only if you don't mind ending up with a loser like my ex. Trust me on this. I know whereof I speak."

He found a station broadcasting a song with a bass-heavy salsa rhythm and settled back against his seat. "How did you make the transition from the loser ex to the air force?"

I heaved a melodramatic sigh. "I wish I could say I was motivated to serve my country. The truth is, holding up my right hand was a direct result of walking in on my ex doing the dirty with our top-heavy neighbor."

"He has to be some kind of stupid."

THE look that accompanied his comment/compliment stayed with me during a brief breakfast stop and the rest of the drive into Tucson. We hit the city outskirts right around nine-thirty.

If you've never been to Tucson, you should go sometime. It's a graceful blend of old and new, with lots of Spanish arches and soaring skyscrapers. Not that I'd seen much of either during my one prior visit. That was spent at Old Tucson, the fake town built as a western movie set way back when and now a major tourist attraction.

Which reminds me . . . I still have one of those old-timey photographs of Charlie and me somewhere. He's dressed up like Burt Lancaster in *Gunfight at the O.K. Corral.* I'm a saloon girl. Naturally.

I made a mental note to dig out the photograph for a ceremonial burning as I followed the directions I'd Map-Quested to B&R Systems Corporate Headquarters. The route took us past sprawling Davis-Monthan AFB, home to the 355th Tac Fighter Wing and, oh, by the way, the boneyard of the air force. I have no idea how many air- and spacecraft are mothballed there in the hot, dry desert sun but it has to be thousands. I caught just a glimpse of them parked wingtip to wingtip before we turned south on I-19.

B&R's headquarters was housed in a steel and glass structure in a modern industrial park not far from Raytheon Missile Systems, one of its major customers. We parked in a visitor's slot and made our way up a walkway graced by dancing fountains and tall palms. Our first stop was the guard manning the security desk in the vestibule.

"May I help you?"

"Hope so," Mitch answered.

Sliding a black leather case out of his back pocket, he

flipped it open to display his Border Patrol badge and a photo ID while I rooted around in my pink and green Coach tote for my air force ID.

"Agent Jeff Mitchell. This is USAF Lieutenant Samantha Spade. We're here to see Ms. Joy Bennett."

The guard consulted a computerized visitor's log. "I don't see either of you listed. Do you have an appointment?"

"No."

"I'll call up to her office and see if Ms. Bennett is available."

He hit the keyboard to search for her number, frowned, and tapped a few more keys.

"Sorry. Looks like Ms. Bennett no longer works here."

"Who is—was—her boss?"

"B&R's vice president for operations, Roger Carlisle."

"Is he available to speak with us?"

"Hang on, I'll check."

Ten minutes later, we were issued visitor's badges and escorted by a bright, bubbly junior assistant into the sixth floor suite of offices belonging to B&R's VP for ops. Once there, we sipped coffee and cooled our heels for a good twenty minutes until the intercom buzzed and we were allowed access to the inner sanctum.

"Sorry. I was on a conference call with our folks in Kuwait."

Carlisle came around his desk to greet us. He was a big man. Six-two or -three, with a thick neck, broad shoulders and piercing gray eyes. I guessed his age in the mid-fifties, but I could have been off by a half decade either way. His glance skimmed over my wild poppy tunic before locking on the badge and credentials Mitch displayed.

"What's this about?" he asked, waving us to chairs in front of his desk.

"We wanted to talk to Joy Bennett but understand she's no longer with B&R."

"That's right."

"Why did she leave?"

"Why do you want to know?"

Not a man to mince words, Mr. Carlisle.

"I was part of the initial task force investigating the death of Patrick Hooker and Juan Sandoval," Mitch replied. "I still have some questions that need answering."

His glance arrowed in my direction. "And you, Lieutenant Spade?"

"I found the bodies. And I helped locate the cell phone used for an anonymous call to the man who ambushed Hooker and Sandoval."

"The phone containing a partial fingerprint?"

"Yep."

"The FBI grilled Ms. Bennett about that cell phone. Also about the fact that Hooker had supposedly brokered a deal for a stolen shipment of B&R weapons. Ms. Bennett swore she knew nothing about Hooker or his connection to the missing shipment. She even took a polygraph. The results substantiated her claim."

"What about her lover?" Mitch asked. "The one who gave her a false name and address?"

The VP's lips tightened. "She says she met him at a Chamber of Commerce mixer some months ago. It was a

big, outdoor affair attended by several hundred local big-
wigs, industry execs, defense contractors and uniformed
types from Davis-Monthan Air Force Base. I suppose I
don't need to tell you the name he gave Ms. Bennett doesn't
appear on any of the official guest lists."

The hair at the back of my neck tingled. I couldn't
shake the feeling we were inching closer to the mysterious rogue agent who may have torched my lab.

"Care to tell me why Ms. Bennett is no long employed
by B&R Systems?" Mitch asked.

Carlisle took his time replying. When he did, I sensed
he was choosing his words carefully.

"The decision was mutual. As you can imagine, the
disclosure about her extramarital affair has caused her
considerable personal turmoil."

Yeah, I thought on a silent snort. Getting it on with
someone other than your spouse has a way of doing that.

"Given the circumstances and the ongoing investigation, I felt it necessary to withdraw Ms. Bennett's security
clearance and access to sensitive corporate data."

"Just what kind of sensitive data was she privy to?"

Carlisle cocked his head. "I provided all this information to the FBI and investigators from the Defense Security Service," he said slowly.

"I'm sure you did."

Mitch's bland reply narrowed the VP's eyes. He glanced
at me again and came to an abrupt decision.

"I'm sorry, but I'm afraid I can't discuss this matter
with you further. The FBI requested B&R not release information to outside sources while their investigation is
ongoing."

"We're not exactly 'outside' sources," I countered.

"Then you can get what you need from the FBI."

He shoved away from his desk and rose, a big man making himself look bigger by towering over his visitors . . . until Mitch rose as well and leveled the playing field. If they'd been squaring off for a Tough Man contest, I knew which one I'd put my money on.

To my surprise, Mitch capitulated with an easy nod. "Thanks for your time."

He took my elbow and steered me toward the door. We went through it with me waffling between disappointment that we'd struck out with Carlisle and awareness of a distinct tingle where Mitch's hand made contact with my bare skin. I couldn't help feeling we'd blown our only shot and said as much as we rode the elevator to the lobby.

"How come you caved so easily?"

"I could see we weren't going to get anything from Carlisle. A fired employee, on the other hand, might be more willing to air her grievances."

"Carlisle said the decision for Bennett to leave B&R was mutual."

"I don't think so. Unless B&R writes some kind of morals clause into their employment contracts, which I seriously doubt, an extramarital affair would only make you a security risk if you're desperate to keep the affair a secret. That makes you vulnerable to blackmail."

"Or a pair of pinking shears to the scrotum. Charlie never knew how close he came to singing soprano."

Mitch slanted me a quick grin but continued with his line of thought. "According to Paul Donati, Bennett admitted her affair readily enough. My guess is the last thing she would want with her marriage falling apart is to lose her job and source of income."

"Maybe she recognized that she needed a change of scene. New job. New lover. New life. I speak from experience here, you understand."

"You could be right. Let's track down Ms. Bennett and find out."

I expected him to call a buddy at the Border Patrol and tap into some cop database. As an alternative, I could have activated the locator in my super-sophisticated, DARPA-supplied cell phone. Instead Mitch detoured to a phone bank in the lobby and flipped through the white pages. He was back in less time than it would have taken me to text in Bennett's name. Guess there's still something to be said for good old fashioned low-tech.

He waited until we were out of the building to call Bennett and set up a meeting. It took some heavy emphasis on *Agent* Jeff Mitchell and *Lieutenant* Samantha Spade before she agreed. A short time later, we pulled into the driveway of a two-story adobe.

Joy Bennett answered the door. I'm not sure what I was expecting, but this short, stocky brunette wasn't it. I don't usually stereotype people . . . Okay, I do. All the time. I'll just say Ms. Bennett would have benefitted from some serious eyebrow tweezing and leave it at that.

She scowled at the badge Mitch presented and held on to the door. "I've told you people everything I know. Why are you hounding me?"

"In cases like this, it often helps to have a fresh pair of eyes take a look at things," Mitch returned, pocketing his badge. "May we come in?"

She stood aside grudgingly. I edged past her into a tiled foyer dominated by a massive antique coat rack. Or hat rack. Or hall tree. I'm never sure what to call those stands. This one had a mirrored back, curlicue brass hooks on either side of the mirror and a golf bag bristling with clubs leaning against it.

"In here," Bennett said, waving us into a living room done in desert tones of brown and brown. Not a spot of color anywhere. I felt like an oversize Elton John in my wild pinks and oranges as I perched on the edge of the sofa beside Mitch. Bennett took a chair opposite us.

Mitch explained our respective roles in the sequence of events starting with Patrick Hooker's demise. He also informed Ms. Bennett we'd stopped by B&R Headquarters to talk to her former boss.

"I'm sure Mr. Carlisle filled you in on the whole sordid story," she said bitterly.

"He gave us a few details. And left us with a few questions we'd like to ask you."

"Ask fast. My husband works nights. He's upstairs, and I don't want . . . I can't take . . ." She stopped, dragged in a breath, started again. "I'd like to get this over with before he wakes up."

"If it makes you feel any better, Ms. Bennett, I think you were a pawn in a very dangerous game."

"It doesn't." Her thick, dark brows snapped into a straight line. "I'm not stupid, Agent Mitchell. I realized I'd been set up the first time the FBI came knocking on my door."

Just like John Armstrong Sr. Someone was damned good at pulling strings and manipulating people into ruining their own lives.

"Tell us why you think you were set up," Mitch said.

"Isn't it obvious? I have . . . *had* . . . a key position at B&R. As their senior analyst, I supervised a team that trended every facet of operations."

"Such as?"

She waved an impatient hand. "Major bid preparation and submission. The status of ongoing contracts. Outsourcing to subs. Plant production. Open action items after inspections by DOD, OSHA, ERP, CMA, the NCIP."

Good grief! And I thought the military lived and breathed acronyms.

"Let's focus on plant production for a moment," Mitch said. "I'm assuming your trending data would include dates, times and destination of major arms shipments."

"You assume right."

"I'm also assuming you didn't knowingly share that information with the man you had an affair with."

"Right again."

Some of the bristly hostility went out of her. Sighing, she slumped her shoulders.

"I had my briefcase with me when I met him after work, though. My laptop was inside it. He could have booted it up when I was in the shower. I don't see how he could have pulled off any data, though. He didn't know the password and my company access code."

"Those aren't all that hard for a pro to obtain."

"Maybe. I guess." Her face crumpled. Self-disgust flowed from every pore. "God! I should have known someone like Nicolas Sloan wouldn't, *couldn't*, have any real interest in someone like me!"

"That was the name he went by? Nicolas Sloan?"

She nodded, miserable. "The FBI said they ran the name and the description I gave them. Neither turned up in their system."

"This guy knows how to play the game," Mitch said gently. "He'll be a master at altering his appearance and probably has a half dozen aliases in his pocket. We suspect he may have targeted Lieutenant Spade, too."

Joy Bennett's startled gaze met mine. "Nick seduced you, too?"

I wish! I refused to dwell on how long it had been since *anyone* had maneuvered me into bed.

"We think he torched my lab."

"Is there anything other than a physical description you can remember about this man that might help locate him?" Mitch asked. "Slang he might have used? Tidbits about himself or his past he may have let drop?"

Her hostility gone, Joy Bennett wanted to help. She really did. But the FBI had wrung her inside out and come up empty. The only really interesting tidbit she let drop was when Mitch asked her why she left B&R.

"It was strongly suggested," she replied dryly. "In case you don't know, Elizabeth Channing owns a considerable share of B&R stock."

"The vice president's wife?"

Bennett nodded, and I suddenly understood all the top-down scrutiny on this case. No wonder Dr. J had received a visit from the FBI!

"Mr. Carlisle wanted to minimize the potential fallout of having an employee with access to sensitive corporate data connected to the Hooker case," Bennett said, her mouth twisting. "Even if the connection is just by way of a missing lover and a stolen cell phone."

Mitch probed for a few more minutes before he gave her his card and got up to leave. I passed her one of mine for good measure.

"If you think of anything, anything at all, give one of us a call."

"I will."

He paused at the door. "One last question. Carlisle said you met Sloan at a Chamber of Commerce function."

"That's right."

"Yet his name wasn't on the guest list?"

"No. Roger . . . Mr. Carlisle . . . made a joke of it at the time. Said something to Nick about knowing the right parties to crash."

"Carlisle spoke with Sloan?"

"They were standing together at the bar when I went up to tell Roger one of the Raytheon VIPs wanted to talk to him. They'd just met, there at the bar, and were waiting for their drinks. That's what Roger told me later, anyway." She hesitated, chewing on her lower lip. "I'm sure that's what he told the FBI."

Mitch nodded and thanked her again for her time.

"What now?" I asked when we were belted into the Bronco again.

"Let's have lunch, then deliver the critter you've been hauling around in the rear of this heap.

MY cell phone rang while we were chowing down at an Applebee's I'd spotted near the interstate. I dug it out of my tote and glanced at the screen, but the number was blocked. Praying it wasn't one of my team calling with some new disaster, I flipped up the lid.

"Lieutenant Spade." A faint click told me the line was open. "Hello?"

I heard another click and quickly disconnected. I'd received too many recorded ads and solicitations to listen to a high-pressure salesman right now. If it was anyone else, they could leave a message.

Mitch was quiet for most of the meal. I could tell he was still mulling over our visit to B&R and The Brow, as Joy Bennett would forever remain branded in my mind.

"What are you thinking?" I asked over a shared serving of my favorite, Triple Chocolate Meltdown.

"I'm thinking that when we get back to El Paso later this evening, I'm going to dig into the background of one Roger Carlisle."

I had other hopes for later this evening and wasn't at all sure we'd make it back to El Paso tonight.

As it turned out, I was right. The utter demolition of my Bronco and subsequent hail of assassin's bullets figured nowhere in my plans, however.

CHAPTER THIRTEEN

IT happened about twenty minutes out of Tucson.

We were heading northwest on I-10. I cruised along with only the occasional laconic reminder from Mitch that fines multiplied with every ten miles over the limit.

Our route took us through the heart of the Sonoran Desert. The rolling landscape was dotted with gnarled mesquite, creosote, saguaro and the desert's own ironwood trees. These, I remembered from one of Pen's boring lectures, exist nowhere else on Earth. They grow to about forty feet in height and supposedly live upwards of fifteen hundred years. I'd taken her word on that.

Off in the distance, the jagged mountains thrust their red-rock peaks high into the cloudless sky. On either side of the highway, dry gullies gaped open like hungry mouths.

The mid-afternoon traffic was sparse for such a well-traveled interstate. So sparse, I divided my attention between Mitch and the empty road ahead, with only sporadic glances in the rearview mirror.

I'm not sure when I first noticed the black SUV trailing us. I do remember thinking at one point that the driver couldn't be on cruise control because he maintained the same erratic speed I did and seemed to stay the same distance behind us.

Not until we reached a curve in the highway and I just happened to glance in the mirror did I see the SUV rapidly closing that distance. It was one of those big, heavy monsters that get maybe eight or ten miles to the gallon and was jacked up even higher on oversize wheels.

"What's heavier than lead?" I asked Mitch, keeping a wary eye on the oncoming vehicle.

"Uranium, I think. Or plutonium. Why?"

"You think I have a lead foot? The joker behind me is wearing boots made of solid plutonium."

Mitch twisted around for a look. "Jesus! Idiot must be going close to a hundred."

Even in those few seconds the SUV had gained so much ground that its shiny grille and front end now almost filled the rearview mirror. I kept expecting it to pull out and pass but it stayed right on my tail.

"Dammit! Why doesn't he go around?"

I tore my eyes from the mirror to gauge the road ahead. The oncoming curve was one of the sharpest we'd encountered since departing Tucson. Mid-curve was a bridge spanning a deep gully. I needed to slow down for the curve, but couldn't hit the brake or the idiot almost kissing my rear end would crawl right up it.

Swearing, I flipped on the directionals and moved into

the left lane to let him pass on the right. When he cut left as well and got within inches of the Bronco's bumper, my jaw locked.

"This has ceased to be funny."

I swerved into the right lane again and took my foot off the accelerator. The SUV surged up alongside the Bronc. For a second or two we were door-to-door. I glared up at dark-tinted windows and pried one hand loose from the steering wheel to shoot him the finger. Pretty stupid, I admit, but I was thoroughly pissed by this time.

I didn't transition from pissed to scared out of my gourd until I hit the brake, and he did the same. We were side-by-side again for another couple of seconds.

I caught a swift movement out of the corner of my eye. My heart jumped into my throat when I realized Mitch had hiked up his jean leg and was reaching for his ankle holster. Before he could get to it, the other driver cut the wheel again. His monster SUV sideswiped my smaller, lighter Bronco.

"Shit!"

The ram shoved us sideways, into the guardrail. With the screech of metal on metal shrieking in my ears, I fought like the devil to keep the Bronco from careening through the rail and flying off the bridge into the gully. In sheer desperation, I stood on the brake. The SUV shot ahead while we fishtailed all over the place.

Each swing was wilder and wider and slammed us back against the metal railing. All I could do was try to minimize the arc and keep aiming for the far end of the bridge.

We almost made it. Had only inches to go when the

Bronc plowed through the last stretch of rail and flew over the embankment.

"Hang on!" I shouted to Mitch, like he could do anything else!

He braced against the dash. I hung on to the wheel. The Bronc nose-dived into the steep-sided gully. We plunged straight down, taking out creosote bushes and prickly pear cacti as we went.

Halfway to the bottom, we hit a rock, tipped and rolled. My driver's side door flew open and came wrenching off. On the second roll, something hit me in the face. My tote, I know now, as it flew through the opening.

Even then we might have walked away. We were both strapped in. The seat belts held and the airbags deployed. If it wasn't for that friggin' tree, both Mitch and I might have sustained nothing more than bruises and cuts.

They don't call those suckers ironwood for nothing. When we hit the trunk, it felt as though we'd slammed into a freight train head-on. The Bronco came to a jarring stop that rattled every one of my teeth.

The impact stunned me. I must have blinked out for a few seconds. When the daze cleared, the Bronc was tipped at a precarious angle and I was in the air, hanging by my seat belt. The powdery chemical stink from the airbag burned my nostrils. Something green and leafy tickled my cheek. Horrified, I realized a limb of the ironwood had broken off and speared right through the windshield.

"Mitch!"

I propped a shaky hand on the center console to steady myself and saw he must have slammed into the passenger side window. It had shattered, and blood from a vicious laceration drenched his forehead.

"Mitch! Can you hear me?"

His lids twitched. He tried to shift, and gave an agonized grunt. That's when I saw that the branch had driven right through his shoulder, pinning him to his seat.

"Oh, God! Don't move, Mitch! Don't move!"

I couldn't get to him. The damned tree limb formed a solid barrier between us and my lap belt was about to cut me in half. I wedged a foot against the floorboard to relieve the pressure and called to him in a voice cracking with fear.

"I'm going to climb out and come around to your side. Don't move. Please, don't move."

The driver's side door was completely gone. I got a grip on the frame with one hand and fumbled for the seat belt release with the other. Once free of the shoulder harness, I scrambled out.

My shaky legs crumpled before I could find my footing on the steep embankment. I went down in clump of creosote and banged my head against the Bronco's up-tilted underbelly in the process. Cursing and seeing stars, I shoved upright.

With the low-hanging branches of the ironwood forming a barrier in the front, I staggered around the rear of the vehicle. The back hatch had sprung open on impact and disgorged EEEK. He'd landed some yards away and was lying half in and half out of his foam-padded box.

I had no time to worry about him. Not with the Bronc tipped almost onto its side and Mitch trapped inside. I had to stretch out on the ground to get to him. His eyes were still closed and blood seeped from the cut on his forehead, but it was the branch impaling his shoulder that scared the bejesus out of me.

The only emergency medical training I've received was a Red Cross CPR course in high school and mandatory training for all casino employees on how to use the defibrillators scattered throughout the hotel and playing floor. I had no idea what, if any, vital arteries or organs the branch might have speared through.

Thrusting an arm inside the shattered window, I felt for a pulse. His jaw and neck weren't clammy or cold to the touch and his heartbeat was steady. I prayed that meant he hadn't gone into shock, and withdrew my arm to rip at the sleeve of my gauzy tunic.

The shoulder seams gave, and I folded the bright poppies into a pad that I pressed against the cut on his head.

"Mitch! It's Samantha. Can you hear me?"

His lids twitched again, then slowly fluttered up. He blinked a few times before focusing on my face.

"You . . . okay?" he ground out through gritted teeth.

"I'm fine." I swallowed a huge fur-ball of panic and tried not to let my voice reveal my stark terror. "But you've got a tree branch spearing through your shoulder."

Slowly, agonizingly, he turned his head. The effort curled back his lips and had his breath coming in short gasps.

"First . . . time for . . . that."

I made a sound dangerously close to a hysterical laugh and tried to wedge through the narrow opening. I knew he had a phone he clipped to his waist, but it was under his hip and I couldn't reach it.

"My purse flew through the window when we rolled," I told him, wiggling back out. "I'm going to climb up the slope, find it and call 911. Don't move! I'll be right back."

The gully was so steep I had to scramble up it on hands and knees. The dry-baked earth was as hard as shale. I was bleeding from a half dozen scrapes and cuts when I heard the sound of a car slowing to a halt on the road above.

My first ecstatic thought was that a passing vehicle had spotted the upturned Bronc and stopped to help. Even before I raised my head, though, I knew with sick certainty that when I looked up I would see a black SUV.

Sure enough, it had pulled onto the shoulder of the interstate. I could see the gleaming grille, the darkened windows, the driver who climbed out and walked to the edge of the shoulder.

He didn't look like a cold-blooded psychopath. Not the ones you see in thrillers like *Fargo* and *No Country for Old Men*, anyway. In his neatly pressed dark slacks, open-neck white shirt and tan sport coat, he could have been your everyday, average stockbroker or Realtor.

His gaze went first to the Bronco's underbelly, which was all he could see from his angle. Then he swept the slope.

He spotted me right away. He could hardly miss me. I was crouched on the baked dirt with no cover except a spiny creosote. My eye-popping orange and pink tunic must have stood out like neon against the plant's silvery green.

Our gazes met for a short infinity. I don't know what he saw in mine. Stark terror, probably. I saw death in his.

Almost casually, he reached across his chest. I didn't wait for him to draw out the gun I knew had to be nested in a shoulder harness. With a scrabble of rock and dirt, I lunged back down the slope.

I didn't hear the shot that spit up dirt some yards to my right. Or the one that sent up another puff just a foot away. As I zig-zagged wildly, a corner of my terror-filled brain registered the fact that the shooter had to be using a silencer. The rest of me just wanted to get out of his line of fire!

I flew the last few feet and flattened myself behind the Bronco. Almost choking with fear, I crabbed forward.

"Mitch! We've got company!"

He forced his lids up. "Bastard . . . who . . . rammed . . . us?"

"He's got a gun."

I was breathing so fast I was sure I'd hyperventilate. I couldn't think, couldn't move. All I knew was that we were both sitting ducks.

"He'll come down," I gasped. "Find you trapped like this. I have to . . . I have to lead him away from here."

"No!"

His lips curled back again in that awful rictus of pain. Without moving his upper torso, he contorted his lower.

"Mitch! What are you doing!"

"My . . . Glock."

His eyes squeezed tight. Sweat popped out and mingled with the blood on his forehead. I couldn't even *begin* to imagine the agony he must have suffered as he tried to reach his ankle holster.

I squirmed into the opening as far as I could, straining to help, but a sharp, metallic ping froze us both. A second thud sounded from the Bronc's exposed underbelly. Realization crashed through me with sickening force.

SUV Guy didn't have to come down the slope to finish us off. All he had to do was hit the gas tank. The son of a bitch could incinerate us both in one giant fireball!

When Mitch's pain-glazed eyes locked with mine, I could see he'd reached the same lethal conclusion.

"Go," he gritted through clenched teeth. "Run for . . . cover."

Cover hell!

I didn't argue with him. There wasn't time. But every instinct I possessed told me our only chance—Mitch's only chance—was to lead our attacker away from the Bronco.

I was up and running in the next heartbeat. I cut into the open for a few terrifying seconds to let him get a look at me before plunging the remaining few feet to the dry gulch.

He had to come after me! He had to!

He couldn't stop to search the Bronco or he might lose me.

With those frantic thoughts careening through my head, I hugged the gully's high bank and ran. I got maybe twenty or thirty yards before three loud shots cracked through the air in rapid succession.

I threw myself against the dirt bank. For a panicked

moment, I thought SUV Guy was right on top of me, that he had unscrewed the silencer, that he intended to pick me off right where I was.

"Samantha . . ."

The weak shout seemed to come from a thousand miles away. I almost didn't hear it over the roaring in my ears.

"Samantha. He's . . . down."

Mitch! That was Mitch!

I blinked the dirt from my eyes and scrambled out of the gulch. SUV Guy lay facedown in the dirt not ten yards away. Blood seeped from a hole in the yoke of his sports coat. The top half of his skull wasn't there anymore.

Gulping, I stumbled back to the Bronco and dropped to my belly. I couldn't imagine how Mitch had managed to retrieve his weapon until I saw him slumped against the dash. He'd shoved forward, impaling himself even more, to reach his ankle holster.

"Good shooting," I choked out.

"You led . . . him right . . . into my line of . . . fire."

I didn't think this was the time to admit my only intention had been to lead him *away*, not into the line of fire.

"We have . . . another . . . problem," Mitch grunted.

"What? Oh, God! You're losing too much blood! Hang on. Please, hang on. I'll find my purse and call for help."

"Samantha." He stopped me in mid-scramble. "I smell . . . gasoline."

Now that he mentioned it, so did I. A wave of nausea spewed into my throat as I rushed around for a view of the Bronc's belly.

SUV Guy hadn't hit the gas tank but one of his shots

must have nicked the fuel line. An oily slick had already pooled below the crumpled chassis.

My heart was pounding so hard and loud I almost missed the ominous click-click-click coming from the engine. A whole new terror grabbed me by the throat. I had no idea what was under the hood that might spark a fire but I knew we couldn't stick around to find out.

I was so shell-shocked I just stood there for a second or two, trying desperately to think how I could get Mitch out. My gaze swung wildly to the road above, to the spreading oil slick, to EEEK's shipping container, to . . .

EEEK. I had EEEK.

Faster than a speeding bullet.

Stronger than the Hulk.

More agile than . . .

Oh, shit. Who cared! I rushed back to the passenger side and flopped on my belly again.

"We need to get you out of there," I told Mitch. "Like, fast."

"You go. Call . . . for help."

"I'm not leaving you. I can use EEEK to help me haul you out of the Bronco but . . ."

"Yeah. But . . ."

His pain-filled glance flicked to the branch spearing into him. Another round of clicks penetrated the small silence. Mitch looked me straight in the eye and ground out what we both knew was a certain death sentence.

"There's no . . . time, Samantha. Go up to the road. Flag someone . . . down and call for . . . help."

When I dig my heels in, they go all the way to China.

"We're wasting time. I'll be right back."

I had to drag EEEK out of the half-open crate. Damned thing weighed a ton, but I finally got him upright and propped against the rear end of the Bronco. Praying his circuitry hadn't sustained damage in the crash, I pressed the switch that powered his computers. When the circuit lights blinked on, I sobbed with relief.

Moments later I was strapped in and ready to go. On EEEK's springy foot pedals I ponged over to the open space that used to be the driver's side door and peered down at Mitch.

"Samanatha, get . . . the hell out of . . . here!"

"Shut up and tell me how to do this."

He gave in to the inevitable. Jaw locked, he wrapped a fist around the branch.

"I'll pull . . . this out. You and . . . EEEK will have to haul me up. Ready?"

God, no! I knew what was coming. Praying I wouldn't throw up when he yanked on that branch, I gulped convulsively.

His knuckles went white where he gripped the wooden lance. Eyes closed, jaw clenched, he dragged in a deep breath and shoved his arm forward.

An animal growl tore from deep in his throat. Sweat popped out on his forehead. Then, finally, when I was sure we were both about to pass out, the tip pulled free and whipped against the roof of the Bronco.

The jagged end looked as sharp as a spear point and glistened with blood. More blood frothed from the gaping hole in Mitch's shirt.

"Okay," he grunted, his face dead white. "Let's get the . . . hell out of . . . Dodge."

I reached down with my heart in my throat and the stink of spilled gasoline in my nostrils. It took several tries before Mitch could get a grip on EEEK's composite arms, but we finally hauled him clear of the wreckage. I refused to think about the pain I must be causing him as I dragged him horizontally along the slope.

With every step, my breath razored in my throat and that horrible clicking grew louder and louder in my ears. We'd covered less than twenty or thirty yards when the Bronco went up. The force of the explosion slammed me, Mitch, and EEEK into the ground.

CHAPTER FOURTEEN

I eased out from under Mitch's prone body and unstrapped EEEK. Propped on one elbow, I gaped at the fiery inferno that used to be my Bronco.

First my lab. Now my car. Almost Mitch and me.

A burst of savage rage exploded inside my chest. SUV Guy was damned lucky he was dead! Then I pushed every thought but Mitch out of my head.

Scrambling onto my knees, I rolled him over as gently as I could. I'm understating the case considerably when I say he looked like everyone's worst nightmare. Beneath the dirt and blood streaking his face, his skin was paper white. Blood pumped from the hole in his shirt. But he was conscious, thank God, and even managed a wry grimace.

"That was . . . a little . . . close."

"No kidding!"

Tearing off the remaining sleeve on my tunic, I wadded it and pressed the makeshift pad against the hole. He raised his good arm up to maintain the pressure while I reached for the cell phone miraculously still clipped to his waist. I fumbled the thing out of its case, but my hands shook so badly I hit 912 twice before I got it right.

"This is the 911 operator. What is the nature of your emergency?"

"We've had a car accident. And an explosion. And a shooting."

"Did you say shooting, ma'am?"

"Yes."

"Have you been shot?"

"No, but the guy who fired at us is dead and my friend was seriously injured when our car went off the road. We're on Interstate 10, about twenty minutes north of Tucson. I don't have the exact location. Just look for the black column of smoke."

"We'll take a fix from your cell phone. I have the police and the ambulance on the way, ma'am. Tell me the nature of your friend's injuries and I'll help you assess what kind of first aid to give him until someone arrives on scene."

"He has a laceration on his scalp and a puncture wound in his left shoulder."

"Is the object that punctured his shoulder still embedded?"

"No. We had to . . ."

The screech of air brakes jerked my head up. A semi pumped to a halt on the road above.

"Someone's just stopped," I told the 911 operator. "A trucker."

From this angle I could see only the top part of the cab and silvery trailer, but the driver soon materialized on the verge. After one startled look, he disappeared for a moment. He reappeared with a fire extinguisher and started scrambling down the slope.

"Hey!" I waved both arms to draw his attention from the roaring flames. "Over here!"

THINGS happened fast after that.

The town of Marana turned out to be close enough to dispatch a squad car and fire truck. They arrived with a wail of sirens, followed in short order by an ambulance and an Arizona State Trooper. A rep from the county medical examiner's office showed up while the EMTs were working on Mitch. A crime scene investigation team were the last to descend the slope.

The fact that Mitch carried a badge must have cut through two dozen levels of officialdom. That, or his loss of blood. The lead investigator took an abbreviated statement from him before he let the EMT load him onto a stretcher.

"We'll talk more once you're stitched up," the investigator promised.

The EMTs offered to take me with them but my scraped palms and knees weren't sufficient to extricate me from the scene. The police instructed the EMTs to patch me up enough to provide a more detailed account of what had happened.

"I'll see you at the hospital," I promised Mitch before they carried him up to the ambulance.

I got a bone-crunching arm-squeeze in return. It had to last me through forty-five minutes to an hour of yes, SUV Guy ran us off the road; yes, he opened fire on us; yes, Agent Mitchell fired in self-defense; no, I don't know who our attacker is or why he tried to take us out. Although . . .

"I think he may be connected to the Hooker case," I informed the various investigators listening to me give my statement.

"Hooker Who?"

"Patrick Hooker. The guy who was killed over near El Paso a week ago. The one suspected of selling stolen arms to druggers."

The state trooper scratched his chin. "I thought they arrested someone for that. The father of a dead marine."

"They did but . . ."

I didn't think I should spill all the details. Particularly since I didn't *know* all the details. Then there was the consideration that both Mitch and I had been told in no uncertain terms to butt out. I didn't look forward to explaining why we butted back in.

"You need to contact Special Agent Paul Donati. He's with the FBI's El Paso office. He knows more about the case than I do."

Mitch's Glock went into an evidence bag. So did SUV Guy's silenced weapon and the bullets the crime scene investigators dug out of the dirt. I should mention that EEEK received more than one dubious glance while all this was going on but they didn't have a bag big enough to stuff him into.

I wasn't surprised to learn SUV Guy carried no ID of any kind. Unless he'd filed, seared or stuck his fingers in acid, though, I was pretty sure his prints would pop up in a database *somewhere*.

He had to be the mysterious, rogue agent who torched my lab. At least I hoped he was. I had no desire to watch any more fires or dodge any more bullets.

Paul Donati and company could work that one out, however. My priorities at this point were to get to the hospital to see how Mitch was doing, then wash away the dirt and smoke clogging my every pore.

Before I could leave the scene I had to figure out what to do with EEEK. That turned out to be a non-issue as the police wanted to impound him as evidence.

I was a tad gun-shy after the loss and/or damage of my lab and associated equipment so I had them write out a hand receipt for Mitch's handgun and for one Experimental Exoskeletal Extension. I didn't care what happened to the smoldering remains of the Bronco.

The state trooper offered to drive me to the hospital. One of the investigators had found my Coach tote with cell phone still intact so I used the drive to call my office. My bandaged hands made dialing tricky, but I eventually got O'Reilly.

"FST-Three."

"Hi, Dennis. It's me."

"Greetings, oh Goddess of Gadgets. Did you deliver EEEK to his makers?"

"Not quite. He's now in the custody of the Marana, Arizona, police department."

"Uh-oh. What happened?"

"Long story. I'll fill you in on the details when I can. Right now I'm in a squad car, en route to the hospital where Mitch is being treated."

"For what?"

"Scalp laceration and tree stabbing."

"Huh?"

"I'll explain later. I just wanted to let you know I may be delayed here in Tucson a day or two."

"Noted. Just out of curiosity, why are you being transported in a squad car? Where's the Rustmobile?"

"Smoldering at the bottom of a ravine."

"Good God!"

I had a mental image of his eyes bugging out below his shock of gingery hair. Pen had once commented that O'Reilly bore a remarkable resemblance to the Kikori River Delta tree frog when startled. I don't have a clue where the Kikori River Delta is, but she nailed the frog part.

"Are *you* okay, Lieutenant?"

"I'm fine except for a few cuts and scrapes."

And a pair of hot pink crops that will never see action again. My now-sleeveless poppy tunic wasn't in any better shape.

"You want me to jump in the van and come get you?" O'Reilly offered.

"Thanks, but I don't know how bad Mitch is or how long we'll be here. I'll rent a car to get us home."

"You don't sound in any condition to drive. Just say the word and one of us will hit the road."

"Thanks, Dennis."

The genuine concern in his voice got me sniffling. For

all their warts and personal idiosyncrasies, my team was . . . well . . . my team.

"I'll call you and let you know what's happening as soon as I check on Mitch."

I hung up, fighting the urge to burst into loud, sloppy sobs. I knew it was a delayed reaction. A cumulative effect. The thing is, I'd never crashed through a guardrail before. Or sailed off an embankment. Or pulled someone out of a vehicle mere seconds before it exploded.

I managed to gulp back the sobs but some watery hiccups must have escaped. The trooper slid me a quick glance and extracted a handkerchief from his hip pocket.

"Here." His expression said he'd seen enough accidents and human tragedy to understand the aftereffects. "Sometimes it helps to let go."

I buried my face in soft white cotton smelling of bleach and sunshine. The combination of those homey scents broke the dam. That, and their reminder that there was a clean, bright world out there untouched by murder or death.

I engaged in a healthy blubber that did nothing for my image as a military officer but relieved a hundred pounds of stress. The handkerchief was a soggy mess when I finished so I stuffed it in my tote.

"I'll launder it and send it back," I promised with a final sniff.

"Keep it."

I was more or less composed by the time he dropped me off at the North Tucson Regional Medical Center emergency room. The intake coordinator did a double take when she saw me. I must have been more smoke-blackened and dirt-stained than I'd realized, as she came out of her chair and rushed at me with a wheelchair.

"I'm okay. Really." I held up my bandaged hands to show I'd already received medical attention. "I need to check on Border Patrol Agent Jeff Mitchell. The EMTs brought him in about an hour ago."

She gave me another, doubtful once-over but went back to her station to consult her computer. "He's still in the ER. Treatment Bay three. I'll buzz you through."

I got the same startled reaction from the ER staff when I hurried down a corridor with squeaky clean white floors and pale green walls. Bay three was near the end of the hall. I rapped a knuckle on the partially closed door but didn't wait for an invitation to enter.

Mitch lay propped at a forty-five-degree angle. An IV snaked from his arm. Monitors beeped above his head. Bandages covered most of his immobilized left shoulder, but his eyes were clear and focused.

"How do you feel?"

"I'll live," he replied with a good attempt at a smile. "How about you?"

"Ditto." I rolled a stool over and plunked down beside his gurney. "What did the docs say about your shoulder?"

"Big hole, minimal damage."

"Don't go all macho on me. What did they really say?"

"That I was damned lucky. The branch speared through muscle and tore some tendons, but missed my lung and brachial artery."

I suspected he was giving me the sanitized version, but a tall, lanky doc in green scrubs entered the cubicle before

I could pry out more detail. Hooking a brow, he ran a quick eye over my bandaged hands and knees.

"I'm Dr. Paulson. You are?"

"Lieutenant Samantha Spade. I was in the car with Agent Mitchell."

"Did the EMTs treat you at the scene?"

"Yes."

"Anyone check your vitals since?"

When I shook my head, he performed a thorough assessment. Only after he was satisfied I wouldn't go into cardiac arrest or bleed out on him did he obtain Mitch's permission to explain his condition to me.

"We ran a series of neurovascular tests. He has good distal pulses in his hands and feet and capillary refill in nailbeds."

Took me a moment to translate that to healthy looking finger- and toenails.

"We irrigated and sutured his wound," the doc continued. "To be on the safe side, we gave him a tetanus shot and put him on antibiotics to counter all the dirt he picked up. Since he lost so much blood, I've set him up for a transfusion. They'll be coming to transport him upstairs any minute."

"Upstairs?"

"It'll take all night to get four units of packed red blood cells into him. We'll keep him in the hospital for at least that long, maybe longer. I've prescribed some pretty powerful painkillers. They'll put him out for most of that time."

A transporter and two ER techs arrived almost as soon

as the doc exited. Mere minutes later Mitch was en-
sconced in a private room and being hooked up to more
tubes. One fed from a bag of the previously mentioned
packed red cells. The thick, dark blood inside the bag
convinced me I had absolutely zero vampire-ish leanings.

I started feeling queasy when the nurse at Mitch's bed-
side asked him to state his name and date of birth and
checked the information against his plastic wristband. She
then read off more data to include his blood type and what
I assumed was his patient ID number. A second RN confirmed the info matched that on the bag of blood.

I don't know why that packaged blood got to me. I had
the real stuff all over me, for God's sake! Mitch's *and* my
own. Another delayed reaction, I decided. But I must have
turned green around the gills since the nurses preparing
the patient suggested I step outside. Mitch was more direct.

"You look like you're about to keel over, Samantha. No
need to stick around the hospital. As soon as they finish
this hookup, I'll call someone and arrange transport for
you back to El Paso."

"Oh, sure. Like I'm going to leave you here."

Kind of hard to carry on a conversation while staring at
the opposite wall, but I managed.

"I'll call my insurance company to tell them about the
Bronco and arrange a rental car to take us both home tomorrow. Be right back."

I could recite a long list of things I dislike about my
present occupation. One of the things I *love* is the mega-
huge USAA Insurance Company that caters exclusively to
military members and their families. When someone clued

me in to the San Antonio–based company, I got them to agree to cover me, the meager personal possessions I'd salvaged from my marriage and the Bronco.

After one call to a USAA claims adjuster and one to Enterprise Rent-A-Car, I had a compact waiting for me at a north Tucson location. The rental office only stayed open until seven P.M., so I arranged to have them pick me up at the hospital in a half hour.

That done, I hit the ladies' room. The first glimpse in the mirrors produced a shriek. No wonder the ER doc had insisted on taking my vitals! I looked like a cross between a grave digger and one of his clients.

I washed the worst of the grime and dried blood off my face, hands and arms before digging in my rescued tote. Fishing out a comb, I gritted my teeth and did battle with my helmet of tangles. My eyes were watering by the time I threw the comb back in the tote and found my lip gloss. Amazing what a swipe or two of Georgia Peach can do to an otherwise scratched and colorless face.

When I ventured into Mitch's room again, his head was back and his hazel eyes were fuzzy. I studiously avoided looking at the slow, dark drip as the nurse informed me she'd administered the painkillers the doctor had prescribed.

"You get some sleep," I told Mitch. "I've got to pick up the rental car and find a place to stay tonight. Then I'll be back to check up on you."

"There's a Holiday Inn Express just across the street," the RN put in helpfully. "They give a discount to folks with family members in the hospital."

"If you have time," Mitch murmured, his voice already heavy and slow, "stop at a Walmart or Academy Sports. I could use some sweats for the drive home."

So could I! My tunic and crops were hitting the Dumpster the moment they came off.

"I'll take care of it," I promised, leaning down to brush my lips over his. "See you in a couple hours."

He raised his good arm and snagged mine. I could see him trying to fight the painkiller's wallop.

"We need to talk about what happened, Samantha."

"We will. Later. Get some sleep."

I'D been operating on adrenaline to that point. Aside from my small meltdown in the state trooper's cruiser, I hadn't really stopped to think about the terrifying experience we'd gone through.

I had plenty of time to do just that while I picked up the rental, made a stop at Walmart and checked into the Holiday Inn Express. Once in my room, I dumped the plastic shopping bags and headed straight for the shower.

With hot water needling into my upturned face and now-aching body, I made myself review the entire sequence of events. From the moment I noticed the black SUV in the rearview mirror to the crash to the shoot-out and explosion.

In retrospect, I saw the hit had been well planned and executed. The bastard had probably tailed us out of Tucson. Maybe all the way from El Paso, although I doubted that. Surely I would have noticed him somewhere along that wide open stretch of highway.

No, he had to have picked us up here in Tucson and followed us out of the city. He'd hung back until we approached the curve in the road, timing his move to send us off the bridge and into the gully. Then he'd come armed to finish us off.

Why?

That question nagged at me as I toweled off and changed into the clean underwear and sweats I'd purchased at Walmart.

Why here? Why now?

If a stone-cold killer wanted to get rid of either Mitch or me, why not do it in El Paso or out at Dry Springs? What did we now know that made us targets?

The only new factor in the equation that I could discern was our unannounced visit to B&R. But the FBI had been there, too. They'd interviewed Roger Carlisle. They'd grilled Joy Bennett. Mitch and I hadn't picked up anything significant from either one except . . .

A sudden frisson rippled down my spine. Gulping, I remembered Mitch saying he was going to dig into Carlisle's background on our return to El Paso.

Carlisle, who'd had a supposedly casual conversation at a bar with Nicolas Sloan.

Carlisle, who'd introduced Sloan to Joy Bennett.

Carlisle, who Joy assumed had told the FBI about his tenuous connection to her lover.

Didn't take a genius to make the next leap. With blazing clarity, I remembered the call I'd received when we'd stopped for lunch. The number I hadn't recognized. The quiet clicks on the other end.

As clear as a bell, I recalled the 911 operator saying

they could get a fix on our location from my cell phone. If 911 could, so could Carlisle. Or Sloan.

Be interesting as hell to see who Carlisle had contacted after we left his office. Paul Donati and company could check that out.

I hurried back to the hospital, anxious to discuss my thinking with Mitch, but he was out cold. I sat with him until the hall lights dimmed and that soft, beeping stillness unique to hospitals descended.

Not until I'd called it quits for the night and started across the street to the hotel did another thought occur to me. Neither Carlisle nor Sloan could know *we* knew they'd had direct contract. The only link between them—and us—was Joy Bennett.

Which could make her their accomplice.

Or as much a target as Mitch or me.

CHAPTER FIFTEEN

I argued with myself for most of the drive to Bennett's house.

She wasn't my responsibility. I didn't owe her so much as a phone call. She'd made her bed, literally and figuratively. Let her sleep in it.

The problem was, I identified with the woman. Not her short, stocky figure, I hasten to say. Or—God forbid!—her beetle brows. But like Joy, I'd let a man make a fool of me. Charlie happened to be my husband at the time, not my lover, but the end result was the same.

Added to that was this gut feeling that Joy might be next on the hit list. Someone needed to warn her, so I'd appointed myself as messenger.

I was just a few blocks away from her house when my cell phone rang. Goosey now over the possibility it had been used to track Mitch and me earlier today, I double-

207

checked the Caller ID screen. I recognized the El Paso area code but not the number. I hesitated, fingering the phone for a long moment before answering.

"Lieutenant Spade."

"This is Paul Donati," a very angry-sounding male barked into my ear. "What the hell is it going to take to keep you out of my business?"

"Excuse me. It's my business, too. Or should I just shrug aside the fact that someone torched my lab and ran Mitch and me off the road?"

"You wouldn't have *been* run off the road if you'd stayed in El Paso and let us work this."

Hard to argue with that.

"I just called Mitch at the hospital," Donati informed me, still steaming. "He was too groggy to talk."

"They gave him some powerful painkillers. He's out for the count. Talk to me instead."

"I'll wait for Mitch to . . ."

My knuckles turned white where I gripped the phone. What did I have to do to gain entree into their friggin' club?

"Talk to me, dammit! I'm as much a part of this investigation as you or Mitch."

Phone to my ear, I waited through a short but speaking silence. Donati broke it finally, his reluctance audible in every syllable.

"We ID'ed the man Mitch shot this afternoon. His name is Edward Granger, although he's used a number of aliases over the years."

"Was one of them Nicolas Sloan?"

"Yes."

I wondered how The Brow would react to discovering she'd jumped into the sack with a cold-blooded killer. That would certainly put a damper on *my* extracurricular activities for the foreseeable future.

"Look," Donati said, breaking into my thoughts, "I can't go into more detail over an open line. Just tell Mitch I'll be up to see him in the morning."

"Before you come, how about checking calls made to and from Roger Carlisle's office at B&R Systems after eleven this morning?"

"Carlisle? Why?"

I turned his question around. "Did Carlisle tell you he knew Granger-slash-Sloan?"

"No. Who says he did?"

"Joy Bennett."

"Why didn't she tell *us* that?"

"Maybe it slipped her mind while you were working her over with a rubber hose."

A pained note came into his voice. "For the record, we don't use rubber hoses on women. Chinese water torture works better with females."

"I'll remember that."

"You should. You keep messing in my business, Lieutenant, and you'll move to the top of my torture list."

He hung up before I'd worked up the nerve to mention that I was about to mess a tad more.

I tucked the phone inside my tote, debating whether I should turn around and scuttle back to the hotel like a good little girl. Donati had sounded half serious with that torture threat.

Then there was my boss. Dr. J, too, had strongly suggested I back off. The fact that I'd helped bring down a killer might win me some brownie points with him, though. If I left it there.

On the other side of the equation was Joy Bennett and my growing conviction she was as much a victim in this whole mess as John Armstrong Sr. Granger-slash-Sloan had destroyed her life with almost as much finality as he'd tried to destroy Mitch's and mine. She needed to be told about her former lover, and that wasn't the kind of thing you dropped on a gal over the phone.

Or so I rationalized as I turned onto her block just in time to see a white sedan backing down her driveway. The sedan jerked to a halt halfway to the street. I did the same two houses away. Her husband, I thought as a male almost as short and stocky as The Brow pushed out of the car. I remembered Bennett telling us he worked nights.

Mr. Brow left the car door open and the headlights piercing the night while he marched back to the two-story adobe. The front door was yanked open before he reached it. Joy stood illuminated in the backlight, her stumpy figure framed against the antique oak coat rack. She gripped the door as her husband launched into a heated monologue, stabbing the air between them with a forefinger.

She obviously didn't care for whatever he had to say. The door slammed in his face a moment later and he stomped back to his car. Tires screeching, he peeled down the drive and whipped onto the otherwise quiet street.

Probably not the best time for me to come calling.

Lips pursed, I debated the matter again before killing the engine. I left the rental parked where it was and walked the short half block to Bennett's house.

She yanked the door open again in response to my knock. Her face was savage with fury, and the golf club gripped in her upraised fist had me taking a quick step back.

"I swear to God, I'll knock you from here to . . . !"

She cut off in mid-shout. Chest heaving, she lowered the club and skewered me with a furious glare.

"What do you want?"

"I need to talk to you."

"I'm all talked out. I'm all *yelled* out. Go away."

She tried to slam the door. Keeping a wary eye on the club, I blocked the door with my foot and blurted out what I knew would grab her instant attention.

"Nick Sloan is dead."

The woman went rigid with shock. In the bright foyer light, I could see the furious red leach out of her cheeks.

"Wh-What did you say?"

"He ran Agent Mitchell and me off the road this afternoon, then used us for target practice. Mitch's aim was better."

"My God!"

She staggered back a few paces. I followed, shutting the door behind me. I didn't intend to leave until I got some answers.

"Did you call Nick Sloan this morning, Joy? Did you tell him that Agent Mitchell and I had been by to see you?"

"No! I haven't seen or talked to him in weeks!"

I believed her. No one could feign that shocked white face and the shaking hand she shoved through her cropped hair.

"Is he . . . ?" Tears leaked from the corners of her eyes. "Is he really dead?"

I was in no mood for nice. "Last I saw of him, he was missing the top half of his skull and being loaded into a body bag. So, yeah, I'd say he's dead."

She dropped the club and let it clatter into the coat rack. Slumping against the foyer wall, she covered her face with her hands. I didn't know whether she was crying for herself or her lover. Both probably.

"Joy, listen to me. I need to know. Did you tell anyone Agent Mitchell and I had come by to see you?"

"My . . . My husband." She hiccuped, dropping her hands. "When he . . . got up."

She lifted a tear-ravaged face. The bitterness and despair that seeped into her expression were painful to watch.

"Your visit this morning sparked a whole new round of arguing. Brian and I have been going at it all day. You just missed him," she added. "He left for work right before you got here."

"Anyone else? Did you tell anyone else?"

"My boss. Former boss," she amended with that awful, aching bitterness.

"You talked to Carlisle?"

"I called him," she said, obviously confused by my sudden, sharp tone. "I wanted to know why he hadn't told you or the FBI that he knew Nick."

"What did he say?"

"That he *didn't* know Nick. He insisted they hadn't exchanged more than a half dozen words that night at the

Chamber of Commerce function. I guess . . . I guess a brief contact like that isn't all that important."

"The hell it isn't."

My vehemence startled her. Blinking, she stared at me.

"Don't you see?" I pressed urgently. "You're the only person who can link Carlisle to Sloan. My guess is he probably freaked out when you said you'd mentioned that link to Mitch and me. That's why he sent Sloan to silence us. Why he might try to silence you."

The blotchy color that had seeped back into her face drained away again.

"You're crazy! Roger Carlisle may be a stinker to work for but he wouldn't . . . wouldn't . . ." She gagged on the word. ". . . *silence* anyone!"

"You've left me no choice."

The terse comment spun us both around. My heart almost jumped out of my chest when I saw Carlisle framed in the door to the kitchen. The gun gripped in his gloved hand didn't do a whole lot for my equilibrium, either.

He wore all black. Black slacks, black leather jacket despite the heat, black knit watch cap pulled low on his forehead.

My heart jackhammering against my sternum, I swiped my tongue over suddenly dry lips and managed what I hoped was a creditable sneer.

"Let me guess. You're all dressed up as a cat burglar because you planned to make this visit look like a robbery gone bad."

"What I planned was to make it look like a case of domestic violence," he ground out.

A muscle ticked in his cheek. It didn't calm my shrieking nerves to realize he was wound tight. Obviously the man wasn't used to doing his own dirty work. I kept my eye on that nervous twitch as he shifted his glance to the woman beside me.

"You set it up for me, Joy. I could hear you and Brian shouting at each other while I waited in the alley behind your house. I'm sure the neighbors could, too."

Bennett had remained mute to this point, paralyzed with fear. Carlisle's utter ruthlessness shocked her into a gasp of disbelief.

"You were going to kill me and let Brian take the blame?"

"Not were. Am. Like I said, you've left me no choice."

His gaze darted back to me. I didn't like the way his mouth went hard and tight.

"Having you here complicates the matter. Freaking Granger. He said he'd take care of you and your friend."

"He tried."

"Where's Mitchell?"

"Outside," I lied. "Waiting for me in the car."

He threw a glance at the window in the room just off the foyer. I used his brief distraction to sidle closer to the golf club tilted against the coat rack. I'd moved only an inch or two when Carlisle's eyes whipped back to me.

"Mitch is armed." I talked fast, my gaze locked with his but every atom of my being focused on that club. "If you shoot us, he'll hear the shots and come in firing. He'll pump a bullet into your head, Carlisle, just like he did Granger."

That shook him. The muscle in his cheek jumped again.

"Granger's dead?"

"Missed that part of my conversation with Joy, did you?"

I used the ruse of thrusting my jaw out to ease another inch toward the coat rack.

"I told her just before you interrupted us that her former lover is now minus the top half of his skull."

"Jesus!"

"The Lord's not going to help you out of this mess, Carlisle. You're hanging out there, all on your own. You might as well give it up now."

"I can't give it up. I'm in too far."

"Listen to me! You don't want to pull that trigger. Even if evidence links you to Sloan and through him to John Armstrong and Patrick Hooker, you can plead to a lesser charge of conspiracy to commit murder. I don't know what penalty that carries in civilian life, but in the military it won't put you in front of a firing squad. At the most you might get twenty to thirty years."

I couldn't believe I was spouting the Uniform Code of Military Justice at the man! All those bored hours perusing the UCMJ and its accompanying Manual for Courts-Martial might just pay off.

I realized I'd overplayed my hand when Carlisle's nostrils flared. "You're forgetting those stolen weapons. That's another ten to twenty."

"You could serve them concurrently," I said, clutching desperately at any legal straw I could pull out of my hat.

"I'm not spending the rest of my life in prison."

I was sure the discussion was over then. I tensed, preparing to leap for the damned club, when Joy distracted us both.

"Tell me something, Roger. If you and Nick were in this together, I assume you were the one feeding him information on B&R's shipments."

"Not just B&R's," the executive admitted. "I tapped into several of our competitor's tracking systems, as well."

"So what did Nick want with . . . ? Why did he . . . ?"

"Go after you?" Carlisle's lip curled. "It started as a joke. You're so straight and sanctimonious, he just wanted to see if he could get into your pants. Once he had, we realized you were the perfect scapegoat if any of this should track back to B&R."

Joy gave a strangled sob and slumped against the wall again. To buy a few more precious moments, I put in my own request for clarification.

"What about Patrick Hooker? Was he a scapegoat, too?"

"Hooker was a problem. We'd heard rumors from sources inside the Justice Department that he was making noises about cutting a deal before his lawyer pushed through that writ of habeas corpus."

There it was again. That "high level" interest. Carlisle must have played his Washington connections for all they were worth.

"We couldn't risk letting him be shipped back to Colombia for trial. Ed assured me their methodology for extracting confessions is considerably more direct than ours."

"Rubber hoses," I murmured, wishing I'd taken Paul Donati at his word and stayed out of his business.

"Exactly. Ed arranged Hooker's escape."

"And subsequent demise. How does it make you feel,

knowing you and Granger played on a father's grief to get him to commit murder?"

His face hardened. "We didn't have a choice."

"Bullshit!"

The explosion came from Joy. Her eyes lit with fury, she shoved away from the wall.

"You made choices every step of the way, Roger. You *chose* to get into the business of selling stolen arms. You *chose* to partner with Nick and this Patrick Hooker. You *chose* to come here tonight."

She took one pace forward for each of her boss's bad decisions, stalking him like a harsh, unrelenting conscience. I held my breath and expected to hear his gun go off at each angry step.

"You made all kinds of choices, Roger. You just made the wrong ones!"

I knew I'd never get another opportunity like the one Joy gave me in that instant. She'd drawn Carlisle's attention, angled him away from me a few precious degrees. In one swift lunge, I got a grip on the club and swung it with everything in me.

The shaft cracked against bone.

The gun flew out of Carlisle's hand.

He doubled over and I swung again. This time the club head connected. I don't think I'll ever hear anything as satisfying as the whack when it hit the back of his skull.

He went down, but not out. Moaning, he tried to get his knees under him.

"Quick!" I shouted to Joy, preparing to wield the club again. "His gun!"

The snick of a round being chambered brought my head

around with a snap. The Brow had taken my meaning literally and was about to pump a round into her former boss.

"Joy! No!"

"You called it," she grated hoarsely. "A robbery gone bad. I had to shoot him. Self-defense."

"Don't do it! He's not worth it!"

"He ruined my life. My marriage."

"You did that yourself."

I can see now that wasn't the smartest thing to point out at the moment. All I can offer in my defense is that I was a leeeetle frazzled.

"If you're going to shoot him," I said with what I honestly intended as heavy sarcasm, "do it because he's a total slime who profits off the pain and suffering of others."

Much to my dismay, I discovered sarcasm rolled off Joy Bennett with the same Teflon ease it did off Pen.

"Good point," she agreed and pulled the trigger.

CHAPTER SIXTEEN

IN one of those ironic twists that life sometimes dishes out, Roger Carlisle ended up in the hospital room right next to Mitch's.

When I arrived at the North Tucson Regional Medical Center early the next morning, the third floor corridor was swarming with uniformed police officers, plainclothes investigators and television news crews. I kept my head down and threaded my way through the milling throng to Mitch's room. I'd given my statement—several times!—to the various law enforcement types who'd responded to Joy Bennett's house last night. I was all statemented out.

I should mention I'd also met Joy's husband last night. He'd raced home in response to his wife's frantic call and barreled his way past the police cordon. I have to admit I sniffed back a tear or two when he opened his arms and Joy fell into them. Sobbing her heart out, she kept crying over and over that she'd been such a fool, that she'd never meant to hurt him, that she would give anything to erase the past.

Speaking from experience I will say it's a kinda tough to erase the mental image of your spouse going all hot and heavy with someone else. I hope Mr. and Mrs. Brow work things out, though. They'd obviously invested more in their marriage than Charlie and I had.

I was thinking about that when I knocked on Mitch's door and stuck my head in. "Morning."

He was sitting up in bed, already dressed in the navy blue sweats I'd purchased in my Walmart shopping spree yesterday. His arm was bandaged to his side, but he looked ready to blow this joint.

"Morning." His hazel eyes tracked mine as I entered. "Hear you had a busy time last night."

"Busy is one way to . . ."

The sight of the thickset male in the chair by the window stopped me in mid-stride.

"Uh-oh."

"Uh-oh is right," Paul Donati growled. Folding his arms across his chest, the FBI agent pinned me with a decidedly unfriendly look. "Care to explain why you didn't bother to mention your planned excursion to the Bennett place when we talked last night?"

"You said you couldn't discuss details of the case over the phone."

Weak. Very weak. But the best I could come up with at the moment. The FBI agent didn't buy it, of course. Beneath his black, wavy hair, eyebrows almost as thick as Joy Bennett's drew together.

"I believe I also told you to butt the hell out of my business."

What's that saying? A good offense is the best defense? Or maybe it's the other way around. Whatever. Aggrieved by his lack of appreciation for my role in busting up a stolen arms ring, I went on the attack.

"Good thing I didn't butt out. If I had, Joy Bennett would be a statistic this morning and you'd have nothing on Roger Carlisle."

"Not quite nothing," Donati huffed. "I checked the phone calls made to and from his office yesterday morning, as you suggested. One call traced to a disposable phone found on Ed Granger's body."

I didn't come right out and crow. I have more cool than that. I let a snickery snort convey my sentiments.

"Have a seat." With a smothered grin, Mitch patted the bed beside him. "Paul was just about to fill me in on Granger."

"He was one of ours," the FBI agent admitted reluctantly as I hiked up on the hospital bed beside Mitch. "He worked for the Bureau for almost a decade before leaving to freelance."

"Like Patrick Hooker," I put in, remembering the information I had Googled up on the former U.S. soldier who'd gone mercenary.

"Like Hooker," Donati concurred. "We know now Hooker and Granger connected while they were hired guns in Iraq. Carlisle came into the picture later, when Granger offered to cut him in on a deal for a shipment of grenade launchers. Carlisle subsequently provided inside data on at least three B&R shipments."

"He said last night he also tapped into competitors' systems."

The FBI agent nodded. "Ms. Bennett gave us that input. Our data systems experts have already alerted several of those competitors. We'll work with them and with B&R to determine how much of their systems have been compromised."

"What's going to happen to Joy Bennett?" I wanted to know. "When I left her place last night, the on-scene detectives were talking possible assault charges."

Especially after The Brow admitted we'd had Carlisle facedown on the foyer floor when she splintered the tile two inches from his face and almost put out his left eye with a near lethal shard. She told the police her intent was to scare him, but she'd never fired a handgun before and didn't know the bullet would ricochet like that.

Personal opinion? Her aim was simply off. Either way, I considered that jagged-edged tile shard minor compensation for Mitch's tree branch.

"We've already nixed any talk of charges against Ms. Bennett," Donati said with a shrug. "They're still pending against you, however."

"*Me?*"

My startled squeak drew a thin smile from the wavy haired agent. His first since I entered Mitch's room, I might add. Raising a hand, he ticked off a daunting list.

"Obstruction of justice. Interfering with a federal investigation. Suborning witnesses."

"You gotta be kidding!"

"You think?"

I angled toward Mitch. "Tell me this guy isn't serious."

"He's not serious."

I don't like being jerked around any more than the next gal but I suppose I deserved a few pulls. I let the agent enjoy a brief gloat, then Mitch keyed in to the aspect of this case that had become so personal for him.

"What impact will the events here in Tucson have on the case against John Armstrong Sr.?"

"Hard to say at this point," the FBI agent replied with blunt honesty. "He did murder two men."

"He was set up, Paul. Just like Joy Bennett."

"I know. I'll talk to the DA. See if we can work some mitigating circumstances.

Donati pushed out of his chair and crossed the room.

"I've got a copy of the statement you gave the investigating officers last night. I've also got Mitch's statement. I may want to talk to you both again. If so, I'll contact you in El Paso."

He shook Mitch's good hand and unbent enough to give me a real smile.

"Think you can make the drive home without sailing off into another gully?"

"I'll give it my best shot."

I had Mitch strapped in and exiting the hospital parking lot when I remembered EEEK. I wasn't up for the drive to Phoenix to return him to his rightful owners, but the least I could do was bail him out of jail.

Okay, okay! You want the truth? The mere thought of another report of loss or damage to property in government custody broke me out in hives.

Mitch had to flash his badge and I had to toss out wholly fictitious facts and figures about DARPA's weight in the civilian community before we sprang EEEK from the Marana police department's evidence locker. To tell the truth, I think the only reason we regained custody was because no one on the police force had any idea how to fire up his computers or what they'd do with him if they did.

His shipping container had been demolished in the explosion so Mitch and I reprised our role as cyborg chauffeurs. We drove back to El Paso with EEEK strapped into the back seat of my rental car.

Our first stop was Mitch's place, where I insisted on putting him to bed and spent the rest of the day playing nurse. Unfortunately, it wasn't the me-doctor, you-hot-hot-hot-nurse kind of play I'd been dreaming about.

Between my periodic checks of his bandages and temperature, we both made phone calls. Mitch, to his supervisor and the assistant DA handling the Armstrong case. Me, to my team and—gulp!—my supervisor.

I won't bore you with the details. Suffice it to say my phone's video screen showed Dr. Jessup round-eyed with disbelief while I recounted my latest series of disasters. His red bow tie bobbed convulsively. Sweat glistened like silver tears against his dark skin.

I hung up convinced he would work either his immediate transfer back to the civilian sector or my immediate transfer back to the air force.

MY gloomy prognostication appeared to come true less than two weeks later.

Both Mitch and I were both back on the job. The hole in his shoulder had healed enough for him to return to duty. My bruises had run the gamut from ugly purple to ugly yellow to gone.

I was in my office on Fort Bliss, struggling to make sense of an invention that purported to transform ordinary grains of sand into acoustical transmitters, when Dennis rushed in.

"You'd better come down to the conference room, Lieutenant. Like, now!"

I'd never seen him so agitated. I was out of my chair before he'd spit the last word out.

"Why? What's happened?"

I had instant visions of Penn stabbing an anti-Global Warming protestor with one of her hair implements or Rocky succumbing to hysterics over a failed test run.

"Just haul your butt to the conference room," O'Reilly panted, already out the door.

I shoved away from my desk and followed him down the hall. Heart pounding, I rushed inside and immediately skidded to a surprised stop.

The room was full. Civilians and military. Army, air force and a few scattered marines. My team stood aligned against one wall. Mitch, Paul Donati and several people I didn't recognize leaned against the other.

The fact that Mitch gave me a grin eased my half-formed fears of another disaster. The sight of Dr. J at the head of the conference table brought them crashing back.

"Sir! What are you doing on Fort Bliss?"

"It's come to my attention that I've been remiss in making visits to my teams in the field."

I wanted to ask what idiot had brought that to his attention. Heroically, I managed to refrain.

"Please come forward, Lieutenant Spade."

I edged past my team, hissing as I went. "What's this about? Any of you guys know?"

Their responses ranged from a stoney look (Sergeant Cassidy) to a shrug (Dr. Rocky) to a nod from Pen and a smirk from Dennis. I blinked twice when I saw EEEK propped in a corner at the front of the room.

Someone—I'll bet my next two paychecks it was O'Reilly and his warped sense of humor!—had arranged EEEK in the pose I remembered all too well. One metallic ankle was hooked nonchalantly over the other. His composite arms were crossed. An air force flight cap tilted at a jaunty angle on his electronic brow. A silver eagle was pinned to the cap.

Colonel EEEK. God help us all!

Thoroughly discombobulated now, I joined Dr. J at the podium. Funny. I'd never noticed he's at least four inches shorter than I am. Or that his eyes were the same shade of warm chocolate as mine.

Probably because he'd been sitting down the few times we conferred . . . and usually regarding me with a combination of caution and nervousness. I caught glimpses of both emotions before he turned to address the gathering.

"Ladies and gentlemen, as I'm sure you know, Lieutenant Spade heads up Future Systems Test Cadre-Three, based here on Fort Bliss. FST-Three's mission is to test inventions for the Defense Advanced Research Projects Agency."

My esteemed supervisor paused, cleared his throat, and forged on.

"FST-Three has faced some enormous challenges in recent weeks, including the loss of their lab and most of their test equipment."

I soared between wild hope and crushing worry. Had Dr. J made the trip to West Texas to announce he'd found funding for replacement equipment and FST-3 would soon be fully operational again? Or was he shutting us down?

I was surprised at the hole that last thought punched in my heart. It's true I complain constantly about being deported to the backside of nowhere to work with my motley collection of geeks and eggheads. Also true, said geeks tend to howl with laughter at morning confab when reviewing some of the absurd projects submitted for our review.

Yet I know that deep inside, every one of us on the team nurses a secret hope we might actually contribute a significant enhancement to the safety, security or performance of U.S. military personnel. Why else would we troop out to Dry Springs once a quarter? Why else would we put up with each other's odd and occasionally repulsive idiosyncrasies? Praying for good news, I tuned in closely as Dr. J continued.

"FST-Three also came close to losing its team chief," he intoned solemnly. "That extraordinary sequence of events is why I'm here today. Dr. England, will you read the citation, please?"

Startled, I swung toward Pen. She stepped forward, her sturdy figure draped in its usual layers of natural fibers, and flashed a wide smile.

"My pleasure, Dr. Jessup."

Feet shuffled and shoulders squared as the rest of the people in the room came to attention.

"Citation to accompany the award of the Joint Service Commendation Medal to Lieutenant Samantha JoEllen Spade," Pen read solemnly.

Stunned, I listened while she described in somewhat extravagant terms my actions in helping to uncover and shut down an illegal arms-for-sale operation that crossed international borders.

Only after Dr. J had pinned a bronze medal suspended from a pretty blue ribbon to my breast pocket did he—*finally!*—announce he'd secured another CHU and funding for replacement equipment. FST-3 could truck on out to Dry Springs again in three to four months!

A round of applause followed these momentous announcements. Then Pen invited everyone to FST-3's end of the hall for iced tea and wheat germ cookies.

"You might want to take a pass on the tea," I murmured to Dr. J before he yielded the floor to my co-workers and associates. As they filed past, I shook hands and received hearty congratulations from everyone. Including Paul Donati.

"Look, I know I came down a little heavy at times, Lieutenant."

"A little?"

"Now that the dust has cleared, I've been asked to tell you the Bureau appreciates your actions in breaking this case."

Ha! I just bet they did.

Mitch was the last to approach. We'd seen each other a

couple of times since the shoot-out. Purely platonic visits, given the severity of his wound. Now that he was out of bandages and off painkillers, though, I had great hopes for our next session.

I saw those hopes reciprocated in his grin as he glanced at the ribbon dangling from my breast pocket.

"Nice hardware."

"I think so," I replied smugly.

Laughing, he hooked a finger in the V of my uniform shirt and tugged me close. His lips brushing mine, he murmured an invitation.

"Want to get together tonight for a private celebration?"

"You bet!"

I vaguely recalled one of my instructors at Officer Training School lecturing us on PDA. In military lingo, the acronym stands for Public Displays of Affection. If you're up there in the cerebral stratosphere with Pen and Rocky you might think it refers to Photo-Diode Array.

When Mitch bent and covered my mouth with his, I put my own spin on the acronym. I'll let you figure that one out for yourself.